The Apostle

Daniel Carlson

Copyright© 2022Daniel Carlson

This book is a work of fiction based upon factual and historical events.

9798215902585

Cover by Carl Goodall

Chapter 1

One Sabbath morning over one hundred and fifty eight years ago, the dawn broke through the darkness, spreading its calefacience over the war ravaged border states lying between the armies of Lincoln and Davis.

It was a cool fresh morning that seemed to offer a blessing and a smile from God upon the blood stained soil and the lost souls of the pained and disillusioned.

The tall timbers and long grass lay still and calm, ready for the warmth to inspire new shoots of growth to cover the black powder of wanton destruction.

Over the wide rivers with steep banks and peninsulas swathed in dark green, over the war torn towns, serene and pessimistic for the arrival of a new day, over the ravaged farms and pillaged homesteads and across the charred battlefields where civilisation now ceased, came the deluge of light as the sun rose above the shadows of the distant mountains.

Over the army camps, beyond the mountains, across the wilderness and deserts, the illuminated glow of reassuring radiance continued to spread as if it was bearing a gleam of faith across all forms of life.

Nowhere did it seem more peaceful than on the banks of the

 Cumberland River where the fast flowing current split the small

burgs of North and South Cave.

Frugal of fruit were the surrounding orchards, barren of corn and

feed were the farms and stained with the blood of the young and

the old were the meadows, yet they all seemed a little less

forbidding as the day of worship stirred.

As the hour for the morning service drew near, a drummer from

the Kentucky volunteers took a stand beneath the church steps

to thunder forth his summons.

A call not just for the Puritans whose idea of religion was that of

a lifelong commitment to God and against the flesh of the devil,

but it was also a beat to torment the enemy beyond the wide

banks of the Cumberland who did not have a cleric to forgive

their sins and offer blessings from the book of the Lord.

Soon the town's folk of North Cave and the journeying soldiers of

Kentucky began to gather, grave men, wounded, old and weak

alongside women who displayed pained scars of sufferings from

the long war.

Trudging wearily together, side by side they solemnly gathered, all dressed in sober coloured garb and blood stained blue uniforms.

Young children dressed in their Sunday best were clasped tight by mothers as they faced the unpleasant process of sitting on a pew when they would rather have been playing in the cool shadowed woods where they could forage for berries or bird's eggs amongst the tall trees instead of listening to a two hour sermon which they failed to understand.

Solemn expressions and a lack of any bright coloured attire was customary for the assembly with the exception of a few young maidens whose slim necks and bonnets were tastefully decorated to show the unionist town and the devil that not all were yet fully subdued by the war.

Slowly, the gathering moved along the path, pausing at the gate to read out the names of the missing or dead on the newly hung roster.

Pale faces, impassioned with an undertone of sorrow, scanned the paper which coldly bore the souls of men destined to never return home.

Shrieks, cries and cusses of blasphemy pierced the ears of those in God's garden from the recipients who suffered unbearing pain from the updated list of those sons, fathers, brothers and friends who were destined never to return home.

An orderly queue formed and, passing by the greeting smile of the pastor, the worshipers began to take up their usual religious positions inside the church.

Nodding a welcome as they moved past him, the pastor smiled and clung to his black shawl, knowing he was wasting his time trying to ward off the pain of the demons for most, but he knew inside he did not have the conviction to stop trying and turn his back on God, yet.

As the audience filed through the open double doors they divided equally amongst each side of the aisle with a forewarned concern regarding strange rumours about their once cherished pastor.

As with most buildings in this war-pillaged region, the floor and walls of the church were bare and the pulpit flowerless, simple. Only an hourglass stood beside an open Bible and solitary candle.

Silence and solemnity bestowed upon the congregation as the official party consisting of the pastor and an accompaniment of Union officers from the Kentucky volunteers entered the cramped church.

The officers stood tall, splendidly dressed and almost stately in appearance with ample vestments, embroidered lapels and white gloves.

With their necks stretched and heads held straight, they strode forward with magisterial grace giving little thought to their blooded and ragged subordinates who loitered under the shade of tall oaks on the grass outside.

A rustle passed through the benches as the notable visitors walked the aisle to the front assigned pew, as was the custom for dignitaries. The prominent seats had been reserved.

The audience stole curious glances as officers passed and ignorant children swivelled on the wooden planks, provoking reprimanding shakes and ignominious slaps to the rear of their heads from the elders.

The drumming ceased and the large double doors were closed to block out the brilliance and indicate it was time for the service to begin.

The minister took his place in the pulpit. He was cast in an unusual image for a man of God. He was taller than most, with large framed shoulders from which hung solid arms and huge hands and thick fingers.

Greying temples indicated his age and his face with a large scar and a broken nose told the story of a life far away from the altar and the book of the Lord, yet he had an awe of intelligence and the exquisite sensitiveness and posture of command needed to fulfil his role in the full house of God.

His presence is a rare union of extreme sensibility and strong resolution, without faltering nerve, but behind the steel reserve there was a hidden discord that he was not ready yet to share with his religious compatriots.

Something irked the minister as he stood before the congregation that morning. His jet pupils dilated as he filled his lungs, gathered his dignity and allowed his eyes to meet the gaze of the assembly.

There was no music to help him lead the hearts of the weary in the opening hymn, but loud bellows were heartily sung by all. Then he lowered his face and the scripture readings followed.

Nothing could be more expressive as his voice recited and hailed forth the Puritan divines.

Every word had its meaning, every description formed a picture, and the whole psalms breathed with powerful majestic reverberations even amongst the mournful and hopeless.

Prayers followed, not the endless monologue of the usual clergymen, but a short and direct benediction full of significance and meaning for the townsfolk of North Cave and the soldiers of Kentucky.

Again he lifted his face to the dim light, and he rose to announce another reading from the text, then it became evident he was to preach on a subject which was common to them all.

Composed, he watched the fixed gaze of expectation as he burst forth with the condemnation of the heathen slave owners and the blood stained human traders who bestowed a lifetime of brutal suffering on the once free spirits of the Lord.

He told of the cry that went forth to touch the hearts of the missionaries, abolitionists and fellow citizens who answered God's call to release the chains of brutality and persecution and end the suffering by showing the world there was a better way to treat fellow brothers and sisters.

He praised the men, women and children who kept the torch of John Brown's freedom burning brightly. He paid tribute to the defenders of the faith whose loyalty had robbed them of life and left their loved ones suffering with hardship and grief.

He paused reflectively to acknowledge the enthusiasm he had kindled, a smile curled his lips and a glow of inspiration glistened in his eyes. He wondered if his congregation would be so enthusiastic when his full feelings were revealed.

"And yet we are being disloyal. Even now, as our war cry has been heard by God and the light has been given, now in our day of illumination, the souls of our brothers and sisters across the Cumberland are stained in blood and their homes are engulfed by flames."

Grave and impassioned with a tone of warning and sorrow, the voice of the minister shook the hearts of the worshippers.

"Generation after generation we have lived side by side with the water serving as the only true barrier until now. We have grown up together, our children have played together in the forests and we have fished together in the river, sharing all of our spoils, until now. Until now, we have prayed together under the shadow of death and we have mourned together. Until now."

His eyes narrowed as they scanned across the faces of the confused. "Will you hear me, I beg? Will you help me? I beseech you. Our brothers and sisters, their children, our cousins and our friends are praying in the shadow of death without a man of God to console them, pray alongside them or guide their passage of grief to Peter's door." He lifted his enormous hands and stretched his fingers as he spoke. There was an infinite tragedy in his voice.

Few in the assembly shed a tear for his powerful plea, many faces grew stern, the bitterness and mistrust for the people on the other side of the river could not be softened by just the power of his oratory. The general and his surrounding officers sat erect and indignant as whispers passed from mouths to ears.

Strong and vehement was the minister's plea. His message was for a man of the faith to be sent across the water and fearless was his criticism of the church in its failure and its lack of regard to find and send a replacement for the ill-fated and long departed reverend of South Cave. With the sands of the hourglass almost run out, the sermon was finished and sinking exhausted onto his seat, the minister sat back and allowed the ladies of the sewing club to sing the closing psalm.

As he closed the service and dismissed the audience, slow and lingering were the words of his blessing, as though he was conscious of defeat and mindful that he had unintentionally insulted the visiting fighters of freedom.

The gathering broke with the congregation filtering out with the same solemnity that had marked their entrance. Reaching the open air the shackled children could no longer contain their pent up frustration and they excitedly burst forwards, free from all detaining hands to run wildly and play in the high mid-day sun. Broad mutterings and murmurs could be heard from the departing and well wishing hand shakers,

"A good man, our minister." Remarked one of the sewing club ladies to the general.

"Daring and bold … very bold ma'am." He tilted his head and cast a wry smile.

"Our pastor is a very good speaker." Commented another woman by her side.

"But why does he make such unpleasant demands?" Questioned a confused looking officer.

"God's will is not always easy to accept." The woman replied.

"A simple doctrinal sermon would have strengthened my faith."

Added another soldier who listened to the conversation.

"The Lord chooses to edify us all." She continued her support.

"Such talk makes me angry." Added an elderly man who approached the group. "Missionaries for the rebels! I have never heard of such insanity and hypocrisy. Pure and simple chicanery."

With reddening cheeks, he waved his cane back towards the church doors. "Shot and powder would be a righteous sermon for those over yonder water."

"That was quite a show." Said the general, reaching out to shake the pastor's hand.

"I spoke with honesty." The pastor accepted the hand and returned a smile.

And so the murmurs of disapproval went on amongst the slowly dispersing groups who despised the rebel armies and citizens alike with such an intensity they had never previously imagined.

Amongst them walked the minister, pale and dejected, realising that his sermon had been in vain and he had failed to wilt the stern prejudices of his own people.

Chapter 2

The Reverend Daniel Earl proceeded immediately through the crowd to his home, which was twenty-five yards adjacent to the idyllic church.

Shot glass filled to the brim with whiskey, he dropped dejectedly into the high-backed leather chair to find solace and reflection.

Born into the poverty of mining, young Dan did not follow the tradition of his generation and seek a scholarship born out of hard labour and occupational hazards from deep under the surface of the ground. He fled home when he was sixteen after reading an article in the penny press that glorified the Battle of Palo Alto.

Within a month, he had enlisted in the 4th Infantry and the young naïve Kentuckian was fighting alongside seasoned veterans in the American-Mexican War of 1846.

Impatient and ardent, he hated the routine grind of training exercises, instead preferring the theology of combat, never shirking from advances of lancers, swords, bullets, or cannons. His ignorance and foolhardiness made him brave and fearless, traits which equalled his invincible mindset.

At a stretch, he reached six feet, and he filled a size ten boot.

He was bulky yet quick and he stood his own ground in knuckle fights with the roughest and toughest men of the outfit.

As the months passed his youthful raw mantle began to be displaced with the toughened features and telltale scars of a fighting man, and when the war concluded with victory proclaimed he tried hard to mould himself into new lines of work. Ranch hand, silver miner, coach driver—they all lacked appeal and excitement.

His recklessness and discontent from lack of adventure led him into many petty quarrels with saddle tramps, whiskey swillers, prospectors, and gunslingers as he drifted between trading posts and mining towns in the wilderness counties searching for an unfound aspiration.

It was in the spring of '52 that his future was taken out of his own hands and decided for him. Whilst defending a woman in a drunken brawl against a local bully and loudmouth called Eli Plummets, Dan landed a blow with his huge fist that rendered the trouble causer unconscious. As the night progressed, the injured man's condition deteriorated and he stopped breathing whilst Dan, unaware of his perilous situation, was still loitering with the whores in the bawdy town's only saloon.

Faced with double six shooters, Dan had no alternative but to raise his hands high and surrender to lawmen who had closed in around him.

Without any chance of escape to freedom, a month later he faced trial for the murder of the nuisance and he was sentenced to a future of eight years of bread, rice, and water in the Louisiana State Penitentiary.

Whilst confined behind iron bars and only released for labour with strict and mean hard work, the Lord revealed the path he wanted Dan to tread by dropping into his lap an aged leather-bound pilgrim Bible from a keeper whose devotion to God could not prevent his demise whilst he was in confinement.

With four years left to reflect on his sins with the accompaniment of the tattered Bible, Dan read over the passages of the Testaments with fascination until the ink faded from his vision and he no longer needed the printed letters to recite the religious text. Pressed by fellow inmates to lead daily prayers and conduct sermons for the dead, he soon became known as the preacher and upon his release he stumbled into North Cave to fill the vacancy left by a long since departed pastor.

In the first two years, he was restless, insensitive, and he struggled to settle as just a man of the faith. Simply conducting the work of the Lord was a task impossible for him to abide, and he found himself standing up to the town's aggressors and the wealthy whose enterprises were harvested from the poor and weak.

He was not a natural fit for a preacher and often he fought hard to suppress his curse for adventure amid the monotony of the holy routine.

To the citizens of North Cave, he was an advocate for the righteous and a staunch follower of the law, but unmistakably they could see the scars of an untold story which clearly affirmed that he was a man who could express his persuasions from the book of the Lord or equally with the power of his fists.

Little was known about the large-framed man with black wavy hair, ghostly grey eyes, and sun-stained skin, yet everyone speculated about the journey which led him to their soulless church.

Legendary fables of his exploits were soon exaggerated throughout the schoolyards and saloons alike. His devilment and daring audacity was revered by the young and naïve.

Tongues spread hushed admirations throughout the haberdasheries and mercantiles for his prose and appeal.

His black hair shone like a fabled crown and his steel-grey eyes seemed to enchant women into trances of unspeakable desires. Shootists surmised his draw was as quick as lightning and his aim was deathly sure.

Some said he had hurled men into eternity without a care and others claimed he had turned bank robbers and murderers over to the law in every town from North Cave to San Antonio. He had killed, confirmed the gossipers, but only in self-defence when there was no other alternative solution to be found. He was a cavalier who stood against all evil and he was a minister ordained by God to rid the world of wrongdoers, malcontents, and traitors. Boys acted out his daring feats of bravery, girls fantasised of being saved from Indians by him.

Drinkers, slopers, gamblers, and aggressors all feared him and stayed clear of his shadow. Fables and exaggerations surpassed the truth he preached daily, and to the public he was still a mystery, a ghost, a hero, and yet possibly a villain.

He was not afraid to face a smoking gun and stand up to bothersome non-believers, often staring at death for his beliefs.

He could be an exhibitionist, flaunting with society's well-to-do, and he could tease the sinful into correcting their wicked ways.

All of which was mainly untrue; however, the truth is often dull and so no one sought the truth. Only he, the stranger, knew the truth of his beginnings, his principles, and exactly how he found his way to North Cave.

He was the only one who knew his age, his motivation, and his true name; to the rest he was an enigma whom they called 'Reverend Dan Earl'.

His arrival was befitting of the border state town where nihilism had crept over the community and the fear of being forsaken by the Almighty had all but been cast aside as the avarice of ill-gained fortunes and the manifestation of intemperance ruled the domineering legislators.

The previous pastor's languidness and lack of spirit had been unable to restrain the fevered devilment which spread fast and dared to scorn in the face of the devout. His lacklustre sermons were recited to diminishing clusters and empty pews.

He did little to encourage the few who prayed for a religious resurgence until finally he closed the door on the house of God and drifted away into the faded memory of the desperate faithful.

As time passed the new pastor laboured hard to please and comfort the staunch religious, and with discomfited devotedness he visited the frail and sick, he prayed and read the Bible to the old, the housebound and the dim-sighted with regularity, and slowly, as time passed, he began to reconcile differences and quarrels with commanding conviction and respect.

North Cave's dissuaders eventually fell silent and slowly the pews began to fill, removing the dust of emptiness. Once more the church on the hillside thundered vibrantly with the words of cheer and courage and songs of rejoice.

But the Lord's work strained upon Dan Earl's conscience. At times he wrestled with his own aspirations, doubting within that he was a true believer of any religious faith and just a mortal creature who found solace and resilience by helping the needy get through another day. He pondered long and often, but still his integrity urged him to serve God and deliver God's message to the grateful.

He shrugged slowly off his doubts as his success with the re-establishment of religion soon raised the interests of the far and wide, especially the females of the embroidery and music classes whose interfering but well-meaning virtues impelled them to believe a successful clergyman should be eased from all the acquainted sorrow and associated grief which bound upon him as a consequence of his duties.

The contentment and support they referred to was by the companionship of a dependable female and they took it upon themselves to relentlessly act as matchmakers.

In the eyes of the judgmental elders within the community, the minister could only be fully acknowledged if he was married and so innumerable plots and events were conducted where he was informed that he should no longer be unattached. A relentless and unmerciful pursuit to implement a matrimonial union gathered pace.

Praises, reminders, wishes, and advice were repeatedly sounded in Dan's ears until he grew weary of their desires and he capitulated, finally succumbing to their proposals should they find a suitable prospect.

Simultaneously petitioning Reverend Dan Earl, the graceless old ladies of the communion pressed their opinions upon a gentle young widow they considered perfect for a minister's wife.

Widowed by the Civil War at the age of twenty-two, Annette 'Nettie' Mayers had conducted her mourning of Cyrus Mayers by confining her sorrow within her heart and going about her duties and her work, for Nettie's nature was to subdue the hurt and pain by seeking relief from exhaustion through practical hard work. But with no family for support, she had been reprieved from destitution by the charity of the embroidery ladies and now she felt obliged to respect their wishes.

In the judgment of the embroidery class and the town elders, Nettie was selected as the ideal one for the well-favoured reverend and likewise, they tried to convince the young widow she was the very one for the unmarried man. Diverse insinuations continued and meetings were arranged until both Dan and Nettie began to wonder if marriage was the path that must be followed.

From Nettie's obvious apprehension, Dan slowly began the gentle courtship with an awkward reserve and the demeanour of a man who was sentenced to death.

From his first accompaniment with Nettie, he sensed only reciprocated kindness and a lack of any romantic desire.

Her round brown eyes displayed sorrow and the embarrassed widow was not at ease in the presence of the revered man. Her once fluent eloquence and grace had been banished by her grief and anguish.

Their correlation continued at a slow but respectable pace, and bowing to the congregationalists' ambitions they eventually married, a union based upon a misguided notion of duty.

Dan Earl's sense of commitment was solely to satisfy the needs of his parishioners, but Nettie's obligations were not only to those who helped her but also to aid her own self-preservation.

It was made clear to her that if she did not abide by their wishes and marry the man of their choice then she would no longer receive their charity and her demise would be certain.

Her choice was simple: marry the minister and secure a position in the community or perish in poverty.

To both Dan and Nettie no sense of duty could blind them enough to acknowledge the terrible fact that companionship was not devotion and that all love was absent.

As the months passed Dan knew his new wife could not love him and he knew her thoughts were not for him, but for her young dead soulmate. He knew it was an effort for her to act the part of a wife towards him and sympathetically he restrained from any lusty emotions.

Day by day Nettie suspected his interests lay beyond her reach and any tenderness in his manner towards her came only from compassion and his sense of duty, but not from his love.

He restrained his feelings hoping that she would one day be able to display evidence of love and from that day on he could love her and devote himself to her, should he be given the opportunity.

Mutually they tended to each other's needs, remained private, and portrayed the role of dedicated husband and wife.

On the anniversary of their marriage, Dan had to be additionally attentive to Nettie as her health suddenly failed her. He paid for the doctor who did little but gravely shook his head over her feverish body.

For over a week she had weakened to the point where she could no longer walk without Dan's help and her malady was one of those that defied all treatments and sapped away life with abrupt and deadly force.

Just one week later Dan returned from morning service to see his crippled wife sat by the window where he had left her. Wrapped in a comforting shawl, her pale face stared blankly down the hill towards the wide flowing river which divided the two small towns, North and South Cave.

Kneeling by her side he sighed knowing she was sorrowful as she started south towards the hail and thunder of the deathly battlefields wishing her heart was buried with her dead true love.

Nettie was startled by Dan's appearance at her side and she turned her head quickly from the window. A fierce crimson blotched her cheeks and through her quivering lips she forced a faint smile.

Her welcoming was always genial, but as usual Dan saw in her eyes that her heart was chiding her for thinking of her past husband and being disloyal to the kind man who was now taking care of her.

'God forgive me,' he lipped, hiding his thoughts of self-guilt as he silently confessed. 'How repulsive I must be to her, forcing myself upon her weak soul.' He held her trembling cold hand and smiled into her yellow eyes which were once as pure as snow with striking spheres of chestnut. 'The very soul which had already given its heart to the fallen.' Now watery with red blemishes under which dark circles formed, all alertness had vanished.

Her face was still pretty, but the hue of poppy had faded in her cheeks and her soft radiance had been replaced with a grey damp paleness with scars of purple.

He let her see none of his anguish nor the strain in his voice as he asked her how she felt. Wearily she lied that she was feeling slightly better and she longed for the day when she was well enough to attend his sermons. She apologised for not being able to make the journey across the street to the chapel and she asked him to tell her about the morning service.

He removed his coat, drew his chair by her side and clasped her hand, and began to outline the sermon. He knew her listening was with obligatory force and without free spirit; it saddened him.

He knew that because of her lost love and her unhealed heart it would be impossible for her to believe in his desire to serve God by spreading the word of the Almighty on the south side of the river in the depth of enemy territory and the lair of the southern devils. But he continued on resolutely explaining the full summation of the morning's dissertation. With a saddened ache, he told her how the townsfolk of North Cave had resented his plea to cross the river to pray and offer solace to those who suffered great misery. They could not understand, he bemoaned, that our once friendly neighbours, many of whom are kin, are suffering too with the tyranny of war, but unlike North Cave they have no clergyman to hear their distress, receive their prayers, and console their grief.

He explained to her, "North Cave's ungodly resistance urges my soul to rise up from within, revolt, and hold firm against the bitter prejudices which have set deep. Our brethren are poisoning their once-held beliefs. The kindness and good nature that once thrived within this town is soured." He shook his head. "It wasn't like this before the outbreak of the war. North Cave was not resentful and bitter towards our neighbours across the river.

It was a welcoming and friendly community where both towns prospered in equal peacefulness."

Nettie sighed to compose herself. She drew in breath so much that her chest inflated and her posture enlarged in the chair, but the movement pained her and she exhaled rapidly.

"I am not educated like you in these matters and forgive me but would you not serve God better by preaching subjects close to their own hearts rather than try to explain your vision which they do not and will never understand?" Her face haggard and her hands trembled from the effort required to speak. "Can you not lead them and show them how to live day by day with God through this misery of suffering and torment of this war?"

He closed his eyes, held the lids tight for a few seconds, and drew in a comforting breath. He was not angry, just disappointed. Nettie had the same prejudices he had encountered earlier in the churchyard, albeit spoken more softly with less hatred and less venomous spite.

He understood Nettie, yet he had hoped she would be more forgiving now she was nearing God.

He removed his hand from her cold knuckles and rose to pace the room with impatient steps, his mind occupied with thoughts that the bitter ways which he had once banished from North Cave had now returned.

He knew within the lodgings and saloons the talk would be of discontentment, resentment, and scorn for their once-considered protector. No matter how hard he conveyed his Godly persuasions he could not alter their opinions until the savagery of war was over and a lengthy peace had once more settled across the banks.

Shaking his head and flashing a glance to the heavens, still in his inner soul his conscience would not permit him to fail God's will.

He halted his pondering and stood before Nettie with his arms folded.

"We all have the same Lord and the same God Almighty. We all have the same religious beliefs and the same rights and wrongs are inside us all, regardless of which side of the river we consider home." He cast a glance into the brightness beyond the window and slanted his head towards the river in the distance. "I think it is impossible for me to continue my work here when there are so many suffering less than two days' walk away."

He sighed and turned his face back towards the gloomy room and knelt once more beside Nettie. He placed both his hands gently over her cold fingers. "I have tried so hard to ignore God's will so often with prayers, but I cannot bring myself to avoid their needs too. It is impossible. I cannot ignore God's call for help and allow their pleas only to be silenced by the seal of death."

Nettie shuffled uneasily underneath her shawl and turned her watery eyes away from his penetrating animated gaze.

"At times I do not understand you. The Lord welcomed you into his house and led you to our town to do his work and do it well. Is it not better to do his work faithfully here than fan the flames of the southern devils?"

"Am I not being unfaithful to the Lord? I cannot ignore his message to help lift the curse from our suffering neighbours."

"Do we not suffer?" She pulled her hand free from his touch and slid it under her shawl. "I do not think the people beyond the river bank share our same beliefs. Don't you think God knew best when he sent you here?" Her words were spoken as a whisper and Dan had to crane his head to hear her opinion.

"Wherever you and I have found ourselves in this life, that is where he intended us to be and we should patiently abide by his will and not deter from his original intentions by seeking out unjust adventures."

"I have toiled with the same thoughts too, but day after day, night after night God is calling me to think of all the widows, the fatherless, the orphans, and the grieving parents who will never see their sons return home because the rulers of our land have divided the country. In my dreams I see bloody slaughter.

The suffering of the naïve and the innocent and the pain in my heart warns me what I must do must be done quickly before the devil can unleash irreparable differences that will never be healed."

The burning ardour which had given his voice intensity for his sermon rose again within his words and he noticed his wife cower behind the shawl. He rose from his knees and gently placed his hand on her shoulder.

"Forgive me Nettie. I forgot you are not well enough to talk about such matters. When you are well we can talk again and I promise you I will listen to your sentiments."

He knew she was not going to regain her health and he knew whilst she still pained for her first love she would never understand his concern for the suffering souls on the opposite side of the Cumberland.

He turned towards the door. "I'll prepare us dinner."

She did not respond. He took half a silent step and angled his face to look down at his companion. He knew if she loved him she would have relented to the nature of his beliefs.

"Thank you for listening to me," he finished with disappointment but with honesty. Then, with an afterthought, he turned back and stretched down low enough to kiss her.

Even though intimacy was rare between them he noticed anger in her eyes that recoiled him and he quickly moved his mouth past Nettie's lips to kiss her clammy forehead instead. His words had disturbed her and she failed to hide her distress from his confession.

"Duty," he murmured almost silently as he walked towards the kitchen. "Always duty and never love."

He shook his head knowing he should never have been persuaded to marry a woman who could not love him.

He closed his eyes to ask God to help him be kind to her and ease her through her tortured darkness.

That evening by her side he preached to her slumber a sermon of hardship and kindness. He spoke of patience, avoiding the darkness of the lines from the book, no matter how much heartache lay beneath them with evil deeds, as he tried to enlighten her mood with words of reconciliation and love.

He spoke of how God helps all who are in need and how he heals and strengthens by leading with gentle kindness even in terrible times of trouble when endurance and sacrifice need to be resolute.

He hoped his reading to her breathed of divinity and compassion as he tried to state his genuine sympathy and sincerity for her.

The darkness of the bedroom was only broken by the flickering of a solitary candle. Nettie lay back low on her pillow in a state of delirious slumber. Her face flushed with fever and her long eyelashes wet with tears. She murmured something inaudible and Dan eased over her to make her comfortable. Lowering his ear to her lips he listened carefully as he wrapped snugly the sheets and padded the pillow around her head.

An excited shudder pulsed through him as she mumbled his name.

He held his brace and listened to her as again she unknowingly spoke, but disappointedly and sorrowfully as she spoke again he realised it was not his name she lipped, it was a longing call for her dead sweetheart.

His huge hand which held tight the bed sheets trembled convulsively as an acute pain burned deep within his chest. He gasped and released a breath as the devil poisoned his thoughts and urged him to end her suffering quickly. He felt his uncontrolled hands on her throat and tense around her windpipe. Tears filled his eyes and droplets fell onto the face of the invalid. He squeezed tight and her breathing faltered.

"God help her," he whispered releasing his hands and turning away to wipe clear the tears which blurred his vision. "God help you Nettie. You have suffered enough."

His tears were not born of self-pity, but of sorrow for Nettie's pain and torment for which he could do little to ease.

A tentative knock at the door shook away his moroseness and to his surprise and relief, one of the ladies from the embroidery class visited with the promise of help.

Together they sat beside Nettie in the semi-darkness until late in the evening and noticing the reverend was worn out by devotion and anxiety the old woman insisted he should take to bed and rest whilst she would take his place at the bedside.

At first he refused, but knowing the woman's determination, he relented on the condition that she would immediately call him if his wife's condition deteriorated further.

As the woman smiled with a nodded promise, he withdrew from the bedroom and made himself a temporary mattress in the living room reading chair. Returning and pausing at the bedroom door Dan took another glance at Nettie. She lay with her eyes closed and her jaundiced face sunk into the fresh white pillow.

The bed sheet over her rose and sank from her difficult breathing and sporadically her head turned from side to side whilst she moaned feverish mutterings.

By her side sat her friend, dampening Nettie's forehead and watching her every movement with observant eyes, and with a gentle touch she tried to comfort the ailing woman.

A longing rawness pitied Dan's eyes. 'Poor Nettie. If only my prayers could make her well and happy again.'

Dan's thoughts were of Nettie and his God and he shook his head believing he was to blame for her suffering by not conducting God's will.

An oil lamp sprayed candescent yellow across the living room. Dan looked at his high-backed, leather-worn chair in which lay his discarded Bible. He clasped the book and slumped in the chair, stretching out his legs. He was too distressed to close his eyes and he knew sleep would not come to him, so he opened the book and fingered through the pages, but he knew it was in vain that he tried to interest himself with its verses.

Irresponsive to the storytelling, the grand book had lost its power to interest and distract him from the mental depression that began to vex him as he tried to find peace and solitude.

The call of God's revelations only caused him more despair and misery as he listlessly turned over the pages without reading.

Slamming the leather binding shut, his eyes cast a flicker to another book which had been left beneath Nettie's chair.

He stretched over without rising to press his fingers on the cover and slide the book across the polished wood towards his feet.

Angling the title to the flickering hue he read out the words on the cover: 'Novel by Harriet Beecher Stowe. Uncle Tom's Cabin'.

Recently he had not given Nettie's interests much thought. Attending to her failing health and occupied with the thoughts of his own mission he realised how little time he had given to Nettie's pastime. He opened the book using her page marker and read, using his finger as a line guide in the dim light. Why is life such a mockery of justice and every written tale a tragedy he thought. He rested his head back to try and sleep, his sight was blurring and his thoughts clouding, but still he pondered why human existence was embroiled with unmerciful suffering and endless gloom. Finally, he slipped into a doze, his head falling into the open pages of the book which led to the great Civil War.

Less than one hour later he awoke with a startle as the book slipped off his knee and the hand of Nettie's friend placed upon his shoulder.

"How is she?" he rasped out of his dry mouth not knowing how long he had been asleep. "Is she worse?"

He wiped the tiredness from his eyes with his knuckles.

The woman did not answer, but her solemnity and muted grace gave him the apprehensive answer he feared. Rising from the chair he hastened to the bedroom with light noiseless steps, but at the doorway he paused at the sight of his ghostly wife. He turned back towards the woman and quietly asked her to bring the doctor knowing the effort and cost would be in vain.

The movement of the pendulum on the hall clock seemed to slow, as alone without a prayer to God he watched his wife's agony distress her further. He clenched both his fists hard into a ball knowing that he would never be able to forget the agony of this long drawn-out night.

The scraping of wood indicated the woman had returned with the doctor and the sight of the flushed old man with the black case and stethoscope gave Dan a modicum of hope as fretfully he watched the doctor lean over his patient and put his paltry instruments to work.

He lowered his harried flushed cheeks close to Nettie's face and listened carefully, then raising with a faint change of expression that implied 'death' as clearly as if he had said it, he shook his head avoiding any eye contact with both Dan and the woman.

Packing away his tools, he confirmed they could do nothing but wait for her end to come.

Dan knew the doctor's distinct lack of affability was as a result of his recent sermons and not due to his tactlessness or inapt medical skills.

He was aware the doctor had only come into Dan's house out of necessity for Nettie and not to ease Dan's burden.

Throughout the lingering night, Dan, the doctor, and the woman took turns to comfort Nettie the best they could, but the cool water used to bathe her brow did little to ease her quivering convulsions and spasm outbursts.

At times when Dan could no longer stand the stench of lingering death and to momentarily ease the burden he went outside to fill his lungs with the fresh pine air which scented the breeze as it wafted over the town from the dense surrounding forests.

When he finished fortifying himself at the door his instincts took him back to Nettie's bedside where he read out a few more of Harriet Beecher's words. Wherever he stood, at the door or by her bed, he felt the same helpless sorrow as he waited for the dawn to break.

His entire being was tortured by the pain his wife was suffering and so sensitive were his feelings that they abnormally invigorated his mind and scattered his thoughts. Without concentrating every letter stood out from the yellowish page with a strange vividness and pictorial expression as the story formed in his mind.

He struggled with an acute perception as reality and fiction merged and blurred his thoughts and as the slow night waned he continued to flick over the pages until finally the dawn crept over the spruce-covered hills and shed its orange across the gloomy room.

He stood, as he had for hours, with haggard eyes at the foot of the bed watching Nettie's sleeping face, but now as the daylight slowly brightened to idle the oil lantern he noticed a calmness develop on her face and replace the contortion of pain.

Dan's lungs filled with unexpected optimism. "Do you think she is getting better?" he asked the doctor.

"She will be free from her suffering very soon," he placidly replied, tilting forwards his face to look over his glasses.

Dan realised the end was approaching and Nettie's life would soon be over. It was not long before the unfathomable calmness of death's prelude graced over Nettie and all her agitation vanished leaving a strange serenity to settle upon her.

Dan stepped forward and moved close beside her. He lowered his face to hers to bid her farewell. He noticed her lips move, but she was almost past the power of speech and he failed to hear her words, but staring deep into her greying eyes he believed she glanced a tender and grateful appreciation as a smile gently creased her cheeks.

Now the early morning's brightness began to engulf the room and a fat shaft of light fell direct upon her pallid face. She turned her head towards the gleam, her lips curled and the amber light seemed to restore her natural radiance and actuate her beauty.

Her head raised and she reached out her hand towards the dazzling beam which fell upon her and she stretched open her palm as if she was reaching out to someone.

Dan felt an icy breeze brush the back of his neck and he shuddered.

"Cyrus," she cried out loudly, then the brief sparkle that had shimmered in her eyes vanished and her smile faded from her lips. She gasped one last time and her hand fell limp onto the bed as her final breath rattled slowly out from her throat.

Dan reached out to clutch her hand and bow his head, not to pray, but just to thank the Lord for ending her suffering so quickly and for reuniting her with her true love.

Quickly her skin paled into whiteness and her eyes glazed. She had become cold to the touch as the vibrancy of her soul departed from its shell forever.

"We'll care for her if you wish," the woman broke the silence and whispered. No one mentioned Nettie's final plea. Dan did not answer the woman with words, he simply turned away from the bed, flicked a brief nod, wiped his eyes, and began to leave the room.

Glancing hesitantly back over his shoulder he saw the doctor use his thumb and finger to close Nettie's eyes for the final time and pull the bed sheet high to cover her face. Consumed by grief for the loss of the woman he was never allowed to love, Dan left the house with unsteady footsteps and plunged himself into the dense woods at the rear of his small garden.

There at the base of a trunk of a wide pine, he dropped himself and buried his face in his hands. A raging confusion swept through his mind and his thoughts. His pledge of marriage shrouded over him like a consuming paranoia and every memory of Nettie pulsed back to him filling him with a sense of failure, regret, and self-incrimination.

'I should have been kinder to her. I ought to have treated her with more respect,' he murmured over and over into his tear-flooded hands. 'I should have tried much harder to be kind to her and I should have consoled her in her grief.' He repeated his regretful sorrow.

He had restrained his full adoration for his wife within his heart, only showing tenderness and respectful consideration whilst she struggled with her lingering grief.

Slowly as the minutes dragged his normal calmness began to return and resting his back on the cool bark he fought to regain his senses and compose his breathing.

He shook away the tears and he looked deep into shadowy shafts of the forest, but he saw nothing as the granting of a new day began to energise the Lord's kingdom.

The shimmer of the bold sun glistening on the damp leaves, the piercing rays splicing through the black trunks, the dashing of the foraging squirrels, and the morning birdsong resonating the joy of a new day all failed to interest him; he saw nothing and he heard nothing.

His heart was desolate, empty of everything.

He did not know what to do next and he did not know if he could find the strength and courage to climb into the pulpit to praise and sing as the Lord would expect.

He sighed, he had not been able to love her, but still she had been part of his life for two years. How was he going to fill the void and relieve the heart-piercing and mind-numbing heartache? He shook his head trying to dislodge the unexpected melancholy and depression.

He closed his eyes and held the lids tight until he saw nothing but sheer blackness, then suddenly a vision formed from out of the darkness.

Dismayed he opened his eyes and he shuddered as the picture remained before him. He narrowed his eyes and squinted several times and he shook his head believing the images were a consequence of an oddity born from an over-stressed brain, yet still the vision remained.

In the distance towards the south, he saw a resemblance to a destroyed large wooden bridge which once straggled the wide ravaging blue river and led the way to a settlement of scattered wooden buildings.

He saw houses and cabins deserted of all vibrancy with shutters and curtains blocking out the promise of the new dawn. He saw stores and mercantile traders empty of provisions and he saw the harrowed sullen faces of desolation and lost salvation.

Blowing in the wind and rolling along the edge of the muddy street was a solitary eagle drum and coming over the distant hill a skinny horse pulled a cart which was laden high with supplies.

Suddenly Dan wrenched and felt light-headed, his eyes gaped and he quickly recoiled from the stare as he realised the cart was being driven by the grim reaper, and its cargo was the ashen faces and dangling limbs of young boys, all dripping blood.

He rose to his feet wavering a little, and the vision slowly began to evaporate to reveal the morning's magnificence. Dan's head furrowed and his eyes narrowed as he strained to focus on the last vestiges of the town, but then suddenly a thunderous blast unsteadied his feet and he had to regain his balance by steadying himself against the tree.

The town had vanished and it had been replaced by the hopelessness of a smog-covered field, strewn with slaughter and death.

Moans and screams of the dying, damp with blood, reeled in front of his eyes and he knew this was no normal battlefield, for the slain were youngsters, ignorant of mortal combat. Gunpowder stung his nostrils and smarted his eyes, blurring them with water as the carnage beset in front of him, a green baize stained with the brace of death.

Most lay perfectly still, their bodies displaying the damage of warfare, some still lingered in their death moaning with pain and screaming for God's mercy. To Dan's relief, almost as soon as the apparition appeared it began to fade again and the field of death sank slowly into the shadows, its surface of green and red merging into the dark tall pines. A mist seemed to settle in front of him whilst the vision still faded, he knew it was not the rising morning dew and he felt an irrepressible desire to walk towards it. A mystifying allurement seized him, not to seek out the broken bridge or phantom town, for he knew the bridge was the crossing over the Cumberland and the desolate dwellings belonged to South Cave.

He could not prevent his whole body from being consumed by a paranormal command which pressed him to walk southwards in the direction where he saw the vision. Slowly he stumbled forwards, tripping over exposed roots and damp foliage until he finally forced himself to stop in bewilderment and question his sanity.

'What could the vision mean?' He wiped his brow and combed his fingers through his tousled hair.

A shudder raced down his spine as he thought he may have contracted the fever from Nettie and was beginning to suffer a disorder of the brain.

He drew rapid deep breaths to calm himself and quell his fear and after a minute of pondering the images he began to conclude the prophetic-infused apparitions must have been borne from his current state of punishing sensitivity.

He stared deep into the beyond, doubting his reasoning and wondering about the significance of the visions. He knew this was not the seventeenth century where preachers existed as apostles spreading revelations based on dreams and omens.

He lived in a modern age of science where visions and delusions were scorned upon and considered signs of madness.

However, he could not dismiss the notion that from the vision a revelation had captured his heart, engrossing his beliefs and dictating a meaning to him.

'The Lord has revealed his will to me,' he closed his eyes, tilted his head towards the sky, and clasped his hands together. 'He has confirmed his path which I am to tread.'

Then he dropped to his knees. 'The Lord has taken my wife away to free me so that I can go forth to South Cave and bring peace into the hearts of the suffering and free the souls of the dead and dying. The Lord has shown me the way to my next mission.'

He arose and opened his eyes to the bright blue above the dark timbers. 'I will walk through the storms of fire and hell or perish in my death.' He then re-closed his eyes and bowed his head to commune with God. 'But God's will must be done.'

After the prayer of gratitude for the visions, he walked with a newfound spirit back to his lonely house. As per the custom in North Cave, the curtains had been drawn by the woman and the rooms were void of any natural light. All mirrors had been covered to prevent trapping Nettie's soul and a portrait of Nettie had been laid flat to prevent her spirit from possessing a living person.

Nettie had been washed and dressed in her finest Sunday outfit, and a lock of her light brown hair had been cut and twined for nostalgia.

The old woman from the embroidery class arose from her chair next to the bed and cast a greeting smile towards Dan as he stood motionless with his huge frame blocking the doorway.

In the dimness, she could see his face was as pale as a corpse, but there was a strangeness to his eyes which bore directly at her and his silent manner and fixed concentration uneased her.

"Is there anything I can get you?" she asked nervously, padding straight her crumpled clothing.

Dan remained silent, his lips resolutely set as if his mind was consumed with thoughts of a far distant place. Dismayed and suddenly feeling uneasy by Dan's lack of usual kindness, the woman grabbed her scarf and valise and barged past him to hurry out of the house without speaking another word.

Alone, Dan's obdurate appearance lapsed as sorrow and pity overwhelmed him. His eyes again flooded as he gingerly walked towards the bed to kiss his dead wife's forehead. He then dropped into the chair vacated by the woman and drew himself level with Nettie's stony face.

Sagging back into the padded leather, he relapsed into a deep lamentation and sobbed loudly into his hands.

Chapter 3

A few days after the funeral, whispers of disapproval spread amongst the storekeepers, the loiterers, and the gossipers, who all rallied to unite words of disapproval towards their pastor's call to become an envoy across the water and into the land of the enemy.

In spite of his passionate pleas to his subjects at the service, he was met with the same barrage of vehement disapprovals as he had before, and everywhere he went in the town, detestation was declared to his face, from the town's domestics to blue-clad fighting men.

On the morning of the Sunday service, the small wooden steps outside the church were crammed to capacity. People stood shoulder to shoulder, all eager to vent their protestations should their pastor dare to repeat his appetite for his mission. Today he had chosen not to greet the worshipers as per his normal custom. Reacting to the obvious discord, Dan Earl had decided to prepare himself away from the false gestures and polite greeters and confine himself to the small sacristy at the rear of the church.

Here in solitude, he drew in rapidly repeating short breaths, he braced every muscle, and he paced the small square room until the preaching hour arrived.

Eventually, silence fell on the stern faces, which resembled a court citing council on a convicted criminal. Grave, concerned stares fell upon the would-be condemned man as he entered the full house to determinedly stride the steps to the pulpit.

After the usual preliminaries, prayers, and songs, Dan raised his head boldly high to give a statement of his reasons for wishing to cross the Cumberland and give an oration in the neighboring rebel town.

Obvious to all was the contrast between his expressive enthusiasm and the grim countenances of the cold, unreceptive audience, but with vigorous command and dignity, he continued to convey the gloom and misery being suffered by their innocent cousins.

He bellowed forcefully that the souls of their once-loved neighbors and cousins were perishing, and sons and fathers were being sent into eternal darkness without God's blessing.

Some dissenters grumbled, and he had to raise his voice above the disgruntled moans and yelling hecklers to ordain that it was God's will and desire that he should go forth and administer his holy comfort to the grieving widows and mothers who, up to now, had been deprived of a fitting tribute and a blessing.

It had been sanctioned that he must divide his time between the two towns so he could tend to the spiritual needs of the unblessed.

Angry repeated calls erupted, and threats of exclusion defied the holy orders.

The congregation's will and anger was loud and precise, stay and serve or leave in disgrace as a traitor, never to return.

Reverend Dan Earl remained defiant and, using the capacity of his lungs, he bellowed above the disgruntled outcries.

"I respect and honour the opinions of my brethren, but I must abide by the will of the Lord God Almighty and conduct his business."

Holding his Bible aloft, he stepped down from the pulpit to tread the boards to meet the most vocal face to face. Silence fell.

Some were astounded by his bravery, some considered him a fool, and others were fearful, for they had all heard the tales of violence in a time not too long ago when he held a different conviction.

For the first time since he took up his position in North Cave, he left the pulpit with his eyes fixed directly ahead and trod between the pews to make his exit before the unyielding congregation. Widened eyes gaped, jaws sagged, heads turned away, the silence only being broken by his leather thudding against the wooden floorboards. Towards his rear, muted murmurings began to develop, but no one had the courage or conviction to stand in his way.

Blazing sunlight dazzled those whose eyes had followed Dan all the way to the church door.

Standing momentarily between the frame, they squinted, still dismayed by his admission.

They watched his shadowy figure tilt his head back to the warm rays and expand his chest with the pine scent. He opened his arms as if to welcome a new epoch and held the stance at length.

"He is rejecting his duty."

"We need him here!"

"He will never be welcomed back."

"Foolish wild goose chase."

The disillusionment to his rear began to gain momentum, and the scraping of pews indicated the mob was about to withdraw and follow on behind him.

"God will make his own judgment upon those who abandon his faithful!"

"Traitor!"

Dan expelled a long breath and, without turning, he heeled the door closed behind him to block out the dissent, and then he began to walk the short distance to his home across the deserted street.

He shook his head with disappointment; he knew his decision to carry the gospel to South Cave would not be welcomed by his fellow believers, but he had underestimated their volatile objections and sudden onset of persecution.

Inside, he knew that some of the congregation's anger would not end with just words of disapproval, as many behind the white door that he had just slammed closed had also lost sons, husbands, brothers, and fathers in the unforgiving war, and their mourning would now resonate in the form of bitter anger and resentment.

He expected the loudmouths amongst the elders to increase the agitation until a willing mob was formed, capable of enacting violence instead of simple damning words to end the matter, and so, absolute with his decision and actions, he walked with his back straight and head held high, convinced the mission given to him by God would yield considerations of valiance come his day of judgment.

In his palm he still gripped his old leather-bound Bible, and reaching the small wooden garden that led to his home, he raised the book to his lips and kissed the tanned, worn binding. Then he closed his eyes and tilted his head again towards the sun for a few seconds to pray for the ignorant who had cast him out.

After the pause, he strode on down the path, his face now flushed and his body invigorated by the ardent exaltation which pulsed through his veins, knowing that he was a vessel for God's presence and that he must not delay touching the sorrowed hearts south of the dividing water. There could be no reconsideration, and there must be no delay.

Hurriedly, he rolled his black cassock and gathered a few belongings and necessities.

He scooped a little food to pack in a knapsack and strapped it securely to his back along with a tarp roll, then he reminisced for a moment staring at Nettie's bedside. He reached for the cutting of her hair and slipped it between the pages of his holy manual, and he scanned one last look around all that once was considered precious. Then after another pause of deliberation, he arched down low to slide open the wardrobe drawer.

Setting his eyes upon an old pistol, his fingers feathered across the oak handle, but with a sigh he pulled back his hand and slammed the drawer closed. Then he turned towards the door. He reached for the door handle and sighed again, he closed his eyes once more and clenched his teeth hard whilst banging his fist on the door frame, then after the hesitancy he again returned to the wardrobe to grab the pistol.

Without further hesitation he tucked the pistol tight into his belt and grabbed a handful of shells.

He paused at the hall mirror to set his hat. As he did so, he dragged his fingers down the brand of past violence that scarred his left cheek.

Firming his comfortable wide-brimmed black hat, he hiked the knapsack high on his shoulder and then, with his trusted book clasped tight in his hand, he ventured out of the cabin.

The church opposite was now void of all life, and the unattended door, which had been abandoned in discontented haste, creaked back and forth in the midday breeze.

Hot roasts scented Dan's nostrils as he took his first step onto the wide soily street.

"There'll be no luncheon for you here today, pastor."

Dan angled his head to see his neighbour leaned on the frame of her front door. Mistakenly she had thought Dan was heading towards her gate as he had done for the last two years after Sunday service.

"You hear me!"

He ignored her rejection and smiled at his former friend, then without altering his gait he simply tipped his hat and continued to walk up the hill, albeit with a small hunger pang tightening within his stomach.

Next to his neighbour's house, a small girl stuck out her tongue at him.

'Was only last year I blessed this young child,' he thought, watching the girl's mother drag her by the arm out of view.

There was to be no lingering farewell for North Cave's former much-loved pastor, he knew that, but still he was saddened by how quickly God's followers in this town no longer held any affection towards him or considered him a friend.

He stepped up onto the boardwalk and passed by the dim-sighted woman whom he had often read the scriptures to. She did not raise her head when his tread sounded on the wooden boards as she always had in the past. Instead, her chin remained rested on her chest as she swayed in her porch rocker.

He knew the woman recognised his gait, yet still he gave her a polite acknowledging nod before continuing on.

The ring of Adams's grocery doorbell caused him to raise his eyes from the boardwalk. In front of him, and carrying a basket, stood the woman from the embroidery class, Nettie's friend who had helped him during her final hours.

Turning sideways, she avoided all eye contact and mouthed something inaudible, then tutted loudly, she shook her head and scurried past him.

Returning to face in his direction of travel, Dan heard the scraping of a door lock and he saw the "Open" sign on Adams's door flip over in front of him, preventing him from collecting much-needed provisions.

He shook his head and quietly recited the words of Matthew: 'For I was hungry and you gave me something to eat. I was thirsty, and you gave me something to drink. I was a stranger and you invited me in. I needed clothes and you clothed me. I was in prison and you came to visit me.'

Then he glanced in both directions of the nearly deserted street and crossed the wide mudded thoroughfare to approach a lame veteran whom he had often prayed with whilst he suffered from his wounds.

"Don't see how you can succeed any," the soldier said.

"The Lord will provide guidance," Dan smiled.

"Only two ways over that river." The old man closed his eyes and angled his face to the bright sun. "Go east and you'll be sent back by the Yankees, and go west and you'll be run in by the Rebs."

He then shook his head. "It just doesn't make any sense to me, Reverend," he admitted.

"It's been a struggle for me too, but the Lord has spelled it out clearly to me now."

"You think?"

"When a man's got a calling by the Lord to be someplace, he just has to get up and go."

"Well then just suppose you do make it across the river. Do you think the townsfolk will be holding a welcome party for you? Or a lynching party?"

"Well, I'm figuring it ain't going to be any worse than being here right now."

The soldier's attention had been gravitated beyond the holy man and he looked over Dan's shoulder and down the street.

"Ain't that—" the cripple did not get to finish.

"Sure is," Dan said. "Well, I guess there'll be no return now."

Thick black smoke billowed and swirled in the light breeze around the porch of his home, and then without any warning the front window exploded outwards with a huge gust of expanding flame.

No one seemed concerned, no one stepped out onto the street to investigate, and no one tried to raise an alarm or to douse the fast-spreading furnace.

Dan's demeanor announced his disappointment. He turned his back to the blaze and, patting the veteran on his shoulder, he stepped away from the boardwalk towards the corral.

Reaching the corral gate, young Travis Leeming stepped out in front of the town's former reverend to block his advance to the barn door. Linking Travis's arm was his impressionable young sweetheart.

Travis grinned and puffed out his chest. "Nothing in here for the likes of you," he spat.

"Just collecting my horse, Trav, so please just step aside," Dan replied peacefully.

"Ain't no horse here for you," Travis repeated to a chorus of giggles from the girl.

"Your pa's looked after my horse for years, Trav, now step aside so I can collect him." Dan silenced the girl with an indignant glare.

"You're not listening." Travis stepped within a few inches of Dan's face. "It's as I said. There ain't no horse here for you."

"He's here alright." Dan remained firm, his eyes transfixed on the shorter man. "I know it for sure."

"Maybe the Lord's taken him," Travis sniggered, then he spat phlegm in the dirt next to Dan's feet. "So just you go and get now. And get on far away from this place as you can b'cos you're not welcome here anymore."

The girl giggled again. Dan's eyes flicked quickly between her and the nuisance.

"When you grow out of your rompers and stand dignified like a true man then maybe, just maybe, you might be able to convince me to alter my ways of thinking. Until then you haven't got the disposition to tell me what I can and cannot do."

Dan leaned forwards to lower his face and level his eyes with the shorter man.

"Romper wearers don't stock these," Travis threatened, sliding open his jacket to reveal an army pistol. "Now you go and get far away because you'll be needing more than that book to protect you if you don't scoot."

Almost as the last menacing words parted Travis's lips, he was hurled violently to the floor as Dan reacted by swinging his book against his temple with enough spontaneous speed and energy that the Bible's leather rendered Travis senseless. Dan's natural urge was to inflict more pain on the boy, but he drew a deep breath and closed his eyes as he struggled for restraint.

"I've got more than a book should I need it." This time it was Dan who flapped open his coat to proclaim he was prepared to protect himself with a blast of lead if needed.

"Now don't bother me again," he commanded as he brushed past the static girl and stepped over the bleeding and bewildered young man.

With his mount saddled and ready, Dan had one last farewell he could not let pass. Riding down the spruce-splitting path which led to the graveyard at the edge of town, he slid down from leather to kneel beside the new markerless grave. He arched over low and, with water filling his eyes, he kissed the cold sod. "Forgive me," he whispered down into the damp earth. "Forgive me for failing you."

Chapter 4

The wide wooden bridge that had connected the two sisterly towns for over twenty-five years had been ruined by dynamite, which made crossing the raging torrents of the Cumberland impossible. Dan had no option in his pursuit of finding a safe crossing but to continue his ride eastwards into stalwart Union territory.

He journeyed along the side of the line of oaks and pines which marked the trail of the Cumberland, and he passed the caves on the high tree-covered ridge where many decades ago the Paleo-Indians had made camp to protect them from the harsh winters. For a moment he brought to mind enjoyable memories of picnics he had enjoyed with Nettie when they had trekked out to view the ancient murals on the cave walls.

He did not linger to reminisce, and late in the afternoon he encountered a disheartened unit of Union volunteers who were returning north with wounded troops. Trudging back for convalescence, their minds and thoughts shattered and embroiled with the presence of death and suffering beyond the raging divide, at first no one concerned themselves with the solitary clergyman.

One by one they passed him by, bandaged heads hung low, limbs pinned and strapped. The ragged column of bloodstained uniforms moaned and groaned forwards with mutterings of want for hot food and a comfortable bed.

Dan sat silently with his head respectfully bowed as the thin frames of once proud and valiant men, whose lives were now forever scarred with the torment of senseless slaughter, slowly passed him by carrying death upon their grim faces.

"My prayers are with you boys," he whispered as his eyes met with the parched faces of a curious footman.

There was no reply, and the troopers continued on slowly until, "What are you doing this far out of town, preach?" asked a mounted soldier who stood out from the rest of the soldiers by the sparkle of his gold-embossed shoulder insignia, his horse half-starved and raw with bleeding wounds.

"Just doing the work of the Lord," Dan replied with a solemn hush as he studied the brown-stained bandage which covered one side of the officer's face and reduced him to functioning with the use of one eye.

"That so," he sneered. "Where you heading?"

"Town on yonder side," Dan carelessly disclosed with a nod and a responding smile.

"That so, uh." The officer cast an opportune glance towards his aide that had walked up close beside Dan and paused to nonchalantly pat the holy man's calm Morgan.

"And what can the Lord do to help my boys?" He opened the palm of his hand and spread it in the direction of the somber parade behind him.

"Well, he can give them strength through the words of his prayers," Dan pulled out his Bible from inside his coat.

"Oh, I'm sure he can do a little more than that now," the officer turned his horse in a small circle in front of Dan.

"He can give them belief and hope and love," Dan sensed an artificial interest.

"Yes, of course, he can be really smart with his words of wisdom, but I'm sure, positive, he can do even more than offer just words of promise."

The procession had halted and Dan was aware that all eyes were now raised in his direction.

"Especially when he can clearly see his disciples are suffering from the wicked heart of the war," the officer lined up his horse to within a few inches of Dan. "They need more than a few words of comfort."

"The Lord is generous and he will guide them through their sufferings with prayers for forgiveness. He will heal from the inside with an undertaking for reform and amelioration," Dan's bolster was firm and loud enough for all to witness.

"That so," the officer nodded, narrowing his eyes with a conceited smile. "Well, ain't that reassuring to hear. But I'm afraid right fine and dandy words ain't gonna cure the pain in their bellies." He turned his eye to look over his shoulder and added loudly, "Is it, boys?"

"That's right."

"Could chew on a rat's ass right now."

"We're just all skin and bone."

"Near on starved to death."

Simultaneous mutterings arose from the many discontented.

"Well, I'm not going to lecture you in profanity, preacher, but you can see for yourself what my boys are needing right now.

Something alimentary to quench their hunger and pain. You see, preach, they ain't gobbled so much as blackstrap in over four days now, and they are well on their way to being keelers."

The sour stench of human rot infiltrated Dan's nostrils as the troopers now gathered in tight around the stationary horses.

"Now the good Lord wouldn't want that now, would he?" The officer seemed to taunt. "More pain, suffering, and loss of precious life."

Dan raised high his sack of rations. "I've only got my pack, but I'm more than willing to share it with you fellas. We can spread it out thin," he offered.

"Now, now. You've got more than that and you know it," the officer removed his hat and wiped his sooted brow with his sleeve.

"What?" Dan blinked with confusion. "I'm afraid I do not understand."

"Don't be a fool, preach!" the officer warned in a sinister tone. "Dismount."

"What? I have nothing of worth and only my knapsack to offer." Dan tightened the reins and considered heeling his horse.

"Do as I say!" commanded the officer with a volley of spittle. "We'll be eating tonight, boys!"

"But I don't—" Dan did not have time to finish his words as his mouth was closed and his vision blurred by the flat steel of the officer's sword as it rapidly cracked against the side of his head.

The Morgan reared in a panic and Dan fell backwards out of the saddle, landing with a brain-scrambling thud. He rolled onto his side and gasped repeatedly, trying to fill his hampered lungs with reviving breaths. He raised onto his knees and managed to clear his vision just enough to see the officer level his pistol to the side of his horse's head, but he did not hear the ear-shattering thud as the crack of a rifle butt to the back of his skull sent him into instant oblivion.

Gradually Dan became aware of the presence of onlookers and he suspected that their deep voices, which were almost lost in an indistinguishable hum, were directed at him. He tried to respond by opening his mouth, but paralysing bouts of pain held him both mute and motionless. He could smell the rank body odour of neglect as someone neared him, and he could feel the warmth of their breath as a face lowered down nearer to his for a closer inspection.

He fought against the pain to crack open an eyelid, but spiralling spasms of excruciation flashed between his temples with a rhythmic cadence that forced him to clamp tight his eyelids in an effort to diminish the imposed pain.

More inaudible comments failed to register his ears, and all of a sudden he felt a prodding in his chest that spread into an all-consuming raging fire of misery that ravaged his every nerve and fibre.

At first, he readily allowed the first vestiges of unconsciousness to relieve the impelling affliction, then as he again began to slip into unconsciousness a deep resentment and anger engulfed his body to trigger a retaliatory response. He drew a lung-bursting breath, shook his head, and cracked open an eyelid.

Shadowy figures circled about him and loomed low above his still crumpled body. Fearing for his life, he clamped hard his teeth to abate the pain just enough to allow him to quickly reach inside his jacket and withdraw his pistol.

An eruption of flash and thunder briefly lit up the darkening sky as he shakily fired off a panic shot above his head.

The sound of iron chains and the rustling of shrubbery accompanied the immediate dispersion of the observers, and within seconds Dan was alone again in the knee-deep foliage.

Trying to glimpse the fleers, he arose too quickly and the blood drained from his head. He swayed, rubbing the lump on the side of his head with his palm, then another intense spasm of pain caused him to collapse again to his knees.

Still unable to recognise what had happened to him, he threw his head back and raged with an agonising loud yell which lasted until his lungs were completely drained of air, and then still in a semi-daze, he scanned the surroundings in the dimming, fluky light.

In the far distance at the edge of the forest, he briefly sighted two half-naked black men, their wide bulging eyes still fixed upon the pained, impaired man, but as they saw him frown in their direction they disappeared into the denseness of the tall barks.

Slowly, Dan began to regain his evenness. He glared in shock at the pistol in his hand, realising his instincts had subconsciously determined his actions. Without fully understanding why, but fearing his life was in danger, he had reached for and fired off his pistol.

Slowly refilling his lungs, he began to remember why he was crumpled on his knees in the damp wild foliage.

His pilfered knapsack lay before him and his Bible just a few inches away where it had been tossed, its pages flickering in the evening breeze. At his side no more than eight paces away lay his dead Morgan, skinned and butchered; all that remained was a skeletal mound of blood and innards.

He dropped his pistol and quickly averted his eyes before shielding them with his hands, but quickly uncontrollable bile rose from deep within and burned his throat as it spurted from his mouth.

He lowered his head and cussed at the Lord for depriving men into desperate savagery, then after a few quiet moments he lifted his head from the cup of his hands and raised himself from the grass.

Firming his unsteady feet he glanced in all directions; all about him was silent and there was no sign of his bedroll or saddle.

His eyes fell upon the Bible and a quiver shot down his spine.

Dropping to his knees, he frantically lunged forward to carefully lock both his hands around the book, then raising it close to his face he flicked through the pages until Nettie's hair fell into his palm. Sighing with relief, he closed tight the remembrance within the pages and reached down to pull a handful of dandelion up to his mouth.

Chewing away the foul taste of vomit, he made his mind up to move on before full darkness descended and the night vultures encircled the carcass. He collected his unraveled cassock and folded it back into his knapsack, then tucking away safely his gun and regretting he had not rested for the night in the caves to the north, he stumbled on until darkness prevented safe travel.

He had cut from the path which he knew the soldiers would have taken, and he moved slowly on between the tall timbers of the evergreens. Resting his back against an enormous fallen tree, he stretched out his sore and aching limbs, then shuffling to improve his comfort, he finally reached inside the knapsack to allow his fingers to fumble through the remnants of his possessions. He turned out the sack onto the grass and in the darkness he could just make out a mouthful of cheese and a half-eaten apple.

The soldiers had left him barely enough food to last out the night. He drew a deep breath and grumbled, then he put the cheese to his lips, but the smell caused him to retract the piece quickly. He still felt queasy from the beating, the sour smell increased his nausea.

Still agitated, he again decided more comfort was needed, so instead of trying to eat he swooped between his arms loose foliage to form a cushion, then sliding down he rested back with his face looking directly at the back canopy of leaves which blocked out most of the moonlight.

The harmony from aroused night creatures prevented any full sleep, and with his mind occupied with the horrors from earlier and his head still pained from the power of the rifle butt, he knew full rest would not come easy.

He tried to heal his aching limbs, but his slumber was soon disturbed when he heard the snap of wood. Keeping his body still, he partially opened his eyes then slowly he wrapped his fingers tight around his pistol and carefully listened.

As he waited for the seconds to crawl into lingering minutes, only wild nature could be heard, but he remained determined to be guarded and vigilant.

Suddenly the foliage close to him shook and very quickly a dark arm protruded through the thick undergrowth, then it withdrew taking within its grasp Dan's knapsack. Dan could do nothing to prevent the theft, but springing bolt upright he levelled out his pistol in the direction of the disturbance and waited.

He squinted in the darkness and listened to clanking of chains and the scurrying of feet trampling in the foliage begin to fade as the thief sped away with his bounty.

Noticing the unmistakable rawness of shackle wounds around the wrists of the arm, Dan knew the fleeing slaves would be desperate for food and once they had emptied the meagre contents of the sack they may return to seek out more, and so to prevent further temptation he fired off another sky-bound warning shot.

The blinding flash and thunder was met with a cacophony of ear-piercing screams and vicious rustling from above as the disturbance unnerved the peaceful nightlife and caused a sudden exodus.

He adjusted to a crouch and listened carefully as the nocturnal stillness returned.

Convinced he was not in danger, he slid away his pistol and clasped his hands to pray for the thief's forgiveness by requesting God to recognise the runaway's desperation and give them a blessing rather than censure for their acts.

Although sore and tired, Dan knew sleep would now avoid him, and so he decided to leave the density of the woods and continue his journey slowly by the guidance of the silvery-cast moonlight.

Soon, dawn goldened the way ahead, and a crude rope bridge showed Dan across the Cumberland and onto the strikingly different terrain. The sloping surrounding fields which led down to South Cave in the distance were nothing but perpetual mud, devoid of all vegetation. Vast parchments blackened where crops once swayed and cattle grazed, but now only windblown ashen dirt swirled above the past fertility.

From the distance, the straggle of wooden buildings which made up South Cave looked unremarkable and void of any prosperity.

Some cabins on the outskirts looked ruined by flame, many others down the distant slope had their doors and windows boarded over with carbon timbers from the torched dwellings.

The streets were empty of all activity, but Dan trod forth with an invigorated pace, his keen gaze locked on the despairing town.

Speculation crowded his thoughts as he studied the abandonment with his squint flickering between the empty corrals and the destroyed stores. He had heard the tales of destitution, and many times through his tormented nightly ritual visions he had seen the destitution, but the sight presented before him still disheartened him.

A solitary silhouette crossing the street paused from their stride and twisted at the hip to look along the sloping track at the approaching stranger in the distance. Dan watched the figure angle his head and use his hand as a sun shield, then after a moment's pause the man began to pace away again with excitable gusto. Even at distance Dan could tell the pygmy figure was suddenly inspired and he assumed it was due to the responsibility of spreading the news of the unexpected visitation.

The mud track meandered through the scorched grass and down the gradient past a small unkempt cemetery, then it dipped across more bare soil until it broadened between the dilapidated facades of buildings which denoted the almost one-street, dust-blown town.

Dan paused at the loose-hanging cemetery gate and looked over the patch with its overcrowded wooden markers and fresh mounds of earth.

A draft of wind followed behind him down the hill and sent a shiver down his spine. The wind continued to bluster and, accompanying the clouds of dirt, a lonely whistle spliced through the gaps between the stores and cabins.

An old man in a rocker cracked an eyelid and arose from his slumber with a stretch and a yawn to watch the man in black pass him by.

"Good morning," greeted the white-collared stranger with a nod.

"Is it?" came the return with a dubious frown.

Dan walked confidently on, soon reaching the centre of the main stretch and the location of South Cave's abandoned church. Besides its almost ruinous state, the church was unusual in the fact that it centred on the town's main street and it was not positioned on the town's boundary like in every other town Dan had visited. He did not dwell on the thought and a faint, but pleasing smile creased his cheeks.

He had arrived at the destination of his calling, and releasing a sigh at the ruinous sight which met his eyes, he shuddered at the challenge which lay ahead.

At first, he quickly examined the lamentable stores surrounding him before returning his surveillance to the forgotten shrine. Roof and wall slats were missing, a sagging door swung back and forth on a creaking hinge, and the entrance had been stripped of steps. The savagery and destitution of war and time had stripped the church and the town of its materials of worth and eroded its former pleasantries.

It wasn't long before doors began to creak ajar, faces parted tattered curtains, and the rise and fall of curious muffled voices swirled amongst the relentless wind.

With his throat swollen with thirst, Dan ignored the interest from the townsfolk and he headed for the well which he saw next to the trough. He spat dust from his mouth and wiped the travel grime from his forehead with his arm, then he arched his aching limbs over the stone coping which contained a bucket and ladle.

He lowered the bucket into the black hole until he heard a light splash echo, then withdrew and sat a while whilst he swilled his face and cooled his throat.

Once refreshed, he looked across the street at the church again. Abandoned and in ruin, it bore the scars of converted stables and what appeared to be grain storage. It no longer thrived in its once-loved glory and only the remnants of a broken wooden cross swinging loose from the door signified the old building was once the town's holy place.

"Can I help you, fella?" shouted a man from a shadow.

"Maybe," Dan turned to address the unknown caller.

"Oh, I see you're a man of God," came the reply.

"Aren't we all men of God?" Dan theorised.

"What you doing here?" The man moved from the shadow to rest on the hitch rail. He removed his small round glasses and wiped them with his fingers.

"Reverend Dan Earl," he replied.

"I didn't ask your name. I asked what your business is here in South Cave."

"Well, I guess to start with I was just hoping you'd allow a friendly fella a sup of your water," Dan raised the ladle and smiled.

"Ah, the Yankee preacher," shouted an approaching burly man. "Kind of wondered if you'd turn up."

"You been expecting me?" A furrow on Dan's forehead displayed his surprise.

"My sister lettered me." The big man hastily sped down the step of the boardwalk to continue his approach. "The dark angel whose creed is to trouble hearts with fear."

Leather on wood sounded as the gathering curious began to step out from behind doors to crowd the surrounding boardwalks.

"To warn us about the preacher with a gun," hollered a woman who had appeared from behind the burly man.

"Get back, woman," raged the man instinctively waving a dismissing arm behind him. "I told you once. This is none of your concern and I'm going to deal with this my way."

"Darn you, Bill Todd! It's him and you know it," she persisted. "Look at the scar."

"Hold your rattle and get back inside," Todd raised his arm suggesting he was going to swing a powerful backhand across the woman's face; however, perceptive to her husband's behaviours, she arched low and twisted away to the boardwalk.

"Darn you. Thinking you can always call the shots."

Dan did not waste any effort trying to figure out who from North Cave had dispatched a letter.

He knew the letter must be true; many knew in days long gone he once concealed his gun under his long coat.

"My name is Dan Earl. Reverend Dan Earl," he said, looking directly at the big man's greasy face. "Ain't it polite in these parts to reciprocate an introduction?" He held out a greeting hand.

"You'll forgive us if we ain't got a welcoming party all prepared, Reverend Earl," said the man leaning on the hitch rail as he replaced his glasses with an accompanying sarcastic slanted grin.

"Beware of the arrival of the devil in sheep's clothing," Todd added, tilting his head and pointing to the letter as if he were confirming a threat. "She advised."

"Maybe she's writing about another visitor." His eyes swept across the expanding crowd of old men, young boys, and women. He saw they had armed themselves, flaunting aged pistols and rusty rifles. "Because I'm pleased to confirm your sister's notion of me is completely wrong."

The big man expanded his chest and positioned himself directly square to Dan's face; a button popped open on his bib-stained shirt.

"Oh no, her words are paired," Todd's eyes narrowed as he examined Dan's face. "The preach with a battle medallion."

He shouted to all around, pointing to validate that Dan's facial scar matched his sister's description.

"Long way from home, ain't you mister?" the spectacle wearer stated.

"My home is wherever the Lord resides," Dan replied, twisting at the waist and opening out both his palms.

"That so." A third man wearing a butternut kepi swaggered onto the street, his thumbs tucked within his belt and his fingers braced across the handles of both his pistols.

"Well, I'll tell it to you straight, holy man. We folks around here don't take kindly to Yankees coming into our parts. God collar or not. It makes no difference to us."

"The Lord doesn't differ between a Johnny and Yank," Dan replied without hesitation.

He did not fear any of the trio and he met their menacing regard with his eyes fixed on the latest intimidator with the sunken cheeks, pallid skin, and war cap.

"Have you got some kind of thinking impediment?" the soldier goaded.

"I am neither mad nor delusional."

"Then what's your business here, preach?" demanded the spectacle wearer with a sinister tone.

"The good Lord has witnessed South Cave's long suffering and torment and he has called upon me to conduct his work in the heartland of this misery," Dan was now face to face with the kepi wearer who had now placed himself determinedly square before him.

"You don't say," he sneered.

"Damn fancy words, preach, but the words of the Lord don't put food in our bellies," added the spectacled man as he walked down onto the street to stand beside his allies.

"Nor bring back our sons, brothers, and fathers," bawled a woman to Dan's rear. A crowd had now begun to gather.

"He can only be commanded through prayers," Dan declared over his shoulder loudly whilst keeping his gaze on the threesome.

"He's just here to gloat at our misfortune," the spectacled man admonished.

"This man is a killer shrouding himself in the mantle of God to hide his sins," the big man shouted volubly using many gestures as he held up the letter from his sister. "Look! All of you. Look." Still holding the paper high to the breeze, he rotated to face the onlookers.

"Look here. Look at the words of my Martha." He swivelled his head to shout to everyone who watched on.

"This man who is claiming a holy revival is an imposter. He holds no papers of holiness from any recognised foundation. He is bereft of God's knowledge and preaches by the ways of the gun. Do not listen to his fraudulent sermons."

"I'm afraid your letter is written with misjudged malice," Dan's reproach was loud and clear. "And it has poisoned your mind with improper preconceived judgments."

"I'm telling you all," Todd's eyes bulged with fury. "This man is the spawn of the devil put on our soil to cause only more pain and suffering amongst the weak and feeble. My Martha is testimony to his pestilence."

"I assure you," Dan calmly smiled and rotated his body to face the gawkers. "I bring no threat or violence. My purpose here is to hear your prayers, restore your faith, and convey the wisdom of the Lord." His words were delivered with an unnerving conviction. "Allow me to deliver the essence of love and forgiveness through the messages of our God Almighty."

"Don't those messages depend on whether you're with Mister Davis or that tyrant Lincoln?" the kepi wearer challenged.

"There is only one union. The union of Christ," Dan halted himself from proclaiming 'that all men are created equal in the eyes of the Lord' in concern his speech would incense the already angered large mob. Instead, he chose to remonstrate with calls of loyalty to God and only God—for peace, love, and forgiveness to all. "The Lord does not look at the things man looks at. The Lord looks into the heart and soul of all."

"Did Eli Plummets' family forgive you when you beat to death their only son, and did the Lord forgive you when you took the life of one of his children!" Again Todd waved the damning piece of paper.

"Forgave—no," replied Dan, stretching out his arms and displaying the flat of his hands to the sky. "Resurrection with new belief... yes. For I was tortured for my sins, but I no longer live that life." His voice was still calm, but loud. "Christ lives within me and I live with the faith of God."

"Bullshit! You're a killer and you'll forever stay a killer," the kepi wearer wrapped his right hand around his pistol. "Your words here are worthless."

Angling his face so that his eyes remained fixed on Dan, the spectacle wearer called out to his fellow citizens. "Now you all listen to me and listen to me good! There shall be no hospitality shown to this man, no gatherings at his behest, and there will be no solace found from his words." He then sneered and spit into the dirt at Dan's feet. "Stand at his side and you stand with the enemies of the North!"

"All I ask is that you stand at the side of our Lord," Dan remained unmoved by the threat.

"We've stood at too many gravesides to rejoice with the glory of God," shouted another woman wrapping her arm around the shoulder of a young boy as she renounced all hope.

"God uses our trials to build our faith," Dan angled to face her. "Draw nearer to God and he will draw near to you. He knows you people around here need to feel the warmth of his embrace."

"Fine words won't prevent another killing," she spat.

"Words are more powerful than any man," Dan continued.

"Not in this town. We don't fight with words," the kepi wearer cut in. "So I suggest you keep on moving, Reverend. Right on down yonder street and back where you came from."

"The Lord has shown me the way here and here he wants me to stay," Dan met the stare of the intimidator.

"Well, us folks around here don't need God's light to show us which path to tread," his fingers tapped menacingly on his pistol.

"There are times when we all need a little guidance," Dan remained calm.

"Well, allow me to offer you some," the kepi wearer now stretched out his fingers.

"Keep it holstered, Flint," the spectacle wearer cut in. "He'll soon scurry back over the water when he realises there is nothing to line his pockets with here."

"And if he doesn't?"

"Then you can take care of him."

"You are mistaken and misguided. I am staying awhile and I am not going anywhere until my work here is done," Dan persisted.

"That so?" The kepi wearer withdrew a pistol and levelled it at the preacher. "Then consider your employ terminated."

"Whoa… hold still there a moment, Flint," the spectacle wearer reached out his hand and carefully placed his palm on Flint Spivey's pistol.

"Not today and not like this." His eyes scanned across the expressionless faces who now gathered inquisitively to form a huge crescent.

"Only the Lord will call in my time," Dan remained unmoved, his eyes focused on the pistol and his nerve unshakable.

"He's a God-darn Yankee just here to lampoon us," Spivey narrowed his eyes, but reluctantly he allowed the press of the hand to lower his pistol.

Dan turned his back to the annoyance of the three men and addressed the crowd. "You are all invited to my first sermon," then he finished by shouting as he walked assertively towards the church. "Sundown tonight."

"The sun will sure go down on you, preacher," Spivey threatened.

Once inside the dark and creaking church, Dan peered out into the brightness. He watched the three men confer amongst themselves with vexed arm wavering and obvious perturbation. They looked in the direction of the church several times before finally gesturing for everyone to return to their business. Dan could not hear their cusses and words, but he knew their message to their fellow citizens was clear.

Chapter 5

The church, bare of any splendor, had been stripped of all valuables and any materials of worth. All furnishings considered salvageable had been claimed and put to use elsewhere.

Bullet-drilled frescoes scarred the woodwork, and the ravaged vaulted ceiling testified to the presence of menacing invaders. Pigeons flapped through the shafts of dim light, and buzzards picked at bones from a carcass in the chancel.

Ravaged many times by skirmishers since the tenure of the last preacher, Dan's initial inspection proved to be correct. Rotten seed and straw showed the building had only survived further pillaging by being made useful as a temporary stable and grain shelter.

After religious abandonment, the locals, who had been left starving and desperate for their own resources and commodities, also selfishly took whatever they could put to use to ensure their own self-preservation and endurance.

Doors, pews, floorboards, and wall slats were missing, and dirt lay thick where once chrismons and ecclesiastical embellishments had decorated the ornate sacrarium.

Dan was invigorated so much by his duties that he was able to ignore the hunger pains and stomach cramps which reminded him he had not eaten, and so, with determination and a strong mindset for resurrecting God's house, he began to clear out the debris, tidy up the wreckage, and sweep out the dregs of disregard.

Soon dusk began to darken the house of prayer, and Dan prepared himself for a narration. He did not need to consult the words of the Bible; he had memorized the Scriptures and so, without any deliberation, he chose to address the distressed natives of South Cave with a message of welcome and forgiveness from Leviticus and Jeremiah.

He stood between the frame of the entrance and waited patiently with hope for an assembly to gather. Gradually the dimness darkened into pitch, and it soon became apparent to Dan that the only gathering to develop was at the far end of the street, where the town's only light emitted a flickering yellow throw.

He twisted his head left and right, but the rest of South Cave was veiled in blackness.

He surmised the lack of illumination was a consequence of war poverty, and those who could not afford oil and candles had taken to their beds.

He drew a sorrowful breath; the town's loudmouths had succeeded with their dissent and no worshipping would be conducted tonight.

He looked again along Main Street. Only two disturbances broke the town's silence. In the distant fields, prairie dogs howled in hunger, and muffled cheer could be detected near the source of the light.

He sighed, but he was not too despondent; he did not expect an easy mission and he knew eventually his actions would be vindicated.

He stepped down into the deserted street and headed in the direction of the activity. His disappointment had permeated into a hunger and thirst which he could no longer disregard, and so he strode with pace and purpose, intent on fulfillment.

He paused briefly in front of the ill-fitting door and looked up at the swinging sign of the Wild Hawk liquor bar. "A drink a dime, a night of shame."

He paused and shook his head on the steps as he listened to the easy talk and bawdy revelers enjoying themselves inside before drawing breath and pulling back the door.

Light, noise, and the rancorous smell of unbathed men and tobacco smoke spilled out onto the boardwalk.

Heads twisted and eyes gazed toward the uninvited intrusion, but without showing any signs of hesitation Dan approached the bar.

The atmosphere within the room was fetid, and the air hazy with the oily fumes of kerosene lamps.

A burly barman with a pitted and knuckle-battered face met Dan at the ale-sodden wooden bar. He dropped his elbows onto the crosspiece and stared as Dan spoke.

"I need a drink."

"There's a well outside," came the reply.

"I need food."

"Then go somewhere else." The tender narrowed his gaze.

Dan looked through the jaundiced light at the curious gazes of the wrinkly-faced, inharmonious revellers, hoping their attention would return to their preoccupations, but silence fell upon the room and the stares remained unabated as they sensed a looming commotion.

"If the Lord wanted me someplace else, He would have beckoned me forth." He met the barman in size and stood face to face, holding without anxiety the inhospitable glare. "And I would have obliged His call without hesitation."

"You'll not find the Lord in here." The barman struck back at Dan's defiance and lifted his elbows to lean on the bar with his huge knuckles.

"And nor would I expect to." Dan's reply was interrupted by one of the drinkers from an obscured position behind crowded shoulders at the far end of the bar.

"Maybe the words of your Lord are clogging up your lug holes, 'cos you ain't listening too good, Reverend."

"Oh, I hear real good, but the will of the Lord is strong." Dan recognised the voice and twisted his waist to face the caller.

"Stronger than lead." Spivey tossed his kepi to the bar and stepped out from behind the gawkers. "You've been told you're not welcome." His courage poisoned by alcohol, he raised his rusty Colt in Dan's direction.

"My place is here," Dan declared, clear and loud.

"Then you'll die here." Brooding for the taste of mindless violence, Spivey cocked the hammer.

"Hold it right there, Flint!" bellowed the barman, holding out his huge palms. "This is my bar and there'll be no killing in here tonight."

"You sure about that, Sam?" Spivey spat back, casting an uncertain whiskey-veined glare.

"My bar, Flint. My rules," Sam replied without hesitation.

"That's a shame, 'cos the way I see it, Sam, if the Lord wants to sacrifice one of His lambs then we should oblige Him." Spivey postured and tottered forward a few steps.

Dan remained fearless. Although he knew Flint Spivey was not bluffing, absolute confidence surged through him. He had glared into the eyes of death many times before, and he sensed tonight was not his time to pass.

Should the Lord not intervene and calm the threat, he had the skills to deal with Spivey, and slowly, concealed by the dull light and smoke, he guided his outstretched fingers towards his gun.

A loud crack shattered the hesitant silence and wind dispersed the smoke as, from his position behind the bar, Sam rapidly swung and landed a wooden baton directly at Spivey's pistol. Without discharge, the Colt thundered to the sawdust on the floor.

"I warned you, Flint!" Sam roared. "If you get the best whisky, it gets the best of you."

"God darn you, Sam." Spivey rubbed his knuckles as he cussed. "This man ain't a man of God. He's the devil's serpent sent to gloat."

"In my bar I do it my way. Now get out! Go home to Helen and sober up," Sam ordered Spivey, then, watching the drunk stumble through the door trying to replace his kepi and pistol, he angled his bulk back toward Dan.

"Now you be warned, devil or God, I worship nor fear neither, and the next time I swing this it will be in your direction." He shook the thick oak club in front of Dan's face.

"So get out of here fast and go find someplace where you're needed!"

Dan's eyes swept across the motionless, wretched faces surrounding him, all of whom offered no support and cast despising glares in return.

Slowly removing his hand from his side, Dan replied, "I return only to the house of my Father where I will lay aside these deeds of darkness and pray for your salvation."

To jeers, laughter, and heckles, Dan turned his back and stepped out into the darkness.

Slamming the door behind him, he immediately became concerned when he glimpsed a moon-illuminated figure glide out from the church doorway and quickly disappear into the blackness.

He squinted and paused momentarily. He wondered if Spivey was hiding in the darkness, but also questioned his sanity.

He was hungry and exhausted and wondered if his eyes and distrustful imagination were conjuring illusions from the shadows of passing clouds.

To quell his alarm as he left the din of the Wild Hawk behind him, he felt the need to rest his fingers on his pistol as he strolled carefully along the centre of the main street and patrolled the front of the church. Quietly and gingerly he placed one foot after the other, but even with care, he could not prevent the creaking boards from announcing his arrival.

He stood at the door of the church and searched the black interior before venturing inside. He refused to withdraw the weapon in God's house, but alert to danger and still expecting to face the drunken gunman, he proceeded forward slowly with his coat pulled back at his waist and his fingers clawed.

All was quiet and still, with the exception of creaking wood, so after a few steps he paused again. Only the sound of his chest rising and falling broke the eerie silence.

Treading stealthily across the loose boards, his attention was drawn to an object placed in the void where the altar had once stood.

With curiosity and still suspecting a trap, he arched over the strange heap to improve his view in the near-blackness, and holding the position, he scanned the church again.

With nothing to concern him, he lowered his face until finally the image cleared enough for him to reach down and touch the outer cloth.

Once more he looked over his shoulder toward the door, then returned to the bundle. He knelt and unfolded the wrapping, and using his hands to assist his sight, his mouth began to water as he lifted from a basket several items of fruit, a bread cob, some dried meat, and a cask. With the cork pulled from the cask and water gushing down his throat, he closed his eyes and thanked the Lord.

Within the calmness of the holy house, relaxation and comfort crept upon him, and exhaustion began to overwhelm him. He stretched out his stiffened, aching limbs and, discharging a spasm of pain, every bone seemed to snap into position.

He shook his head to dispel the sluggishness and tried to rub the tiredness from his eyes with his knuckles as he resisted the strain on his eyelids which threatened to surrender to lethargy.

Suddenly he was stiff and sore in every joint; he was bone weary, yet he could not fully sleep.

He was unable to banish the churning doubts, lingering apprehensions, and thoughts of failure which endlessly needled his slumber and prevented a restful doze.

By the time the sun warmed the tips of the distant mountains and the loiterers were walking off their night stiffness, Dan had scoured the surrounding wasteland and built a sturdy travois which he planned to load with scavenged materials from the abandoned charcoal cabins he passed on the approach to South Cave.

Using stripped bark to secure his first load, by noon he dragged an assortment of charred timbers, branches, and vines through the middle of Main Street.

Curious onlookers paused as wood scraping along the hard dirt intrigued them. Many wondered about the preacher's motivation, some were skeptical and disapproving, but raising his face to offer occasional glances and a friendly smile to the captivated observers, he sensed that a few wanted to ease his solitary struggle. However, alone and onward he dragged his haul of building materials past them all, knowing after yesterday's display of intimidation they would be too afraid to step beyond the porches and hitch rails to oblige their urges.

"Wastin' your time, Yank." Dan saw the spectacled man on the boardwalk shaking his head with a disparaging grin. "Just a-wastin' your time," he repeated.

Continuing on with his body angled low and his head directed toward the dirt, Dan passed the mutterings of disapproval until a pair of leather boots dominated his eyeline and blocked his progress. From his crouched position, he angled his head, allowing his eyes to rise along the legs and body of the man. Although shadowed by the bright high sun, the kepi confirmed to Dan the menace blocking his path was Flint Spivey.

"Why, damn my eyes," Spivey spat.

"I see you ain't heeded your warnings." He turned his head sideways and seized his nose between his thumb and forefinger to blow a large cord of snot to the floor, then wiped his fingers on his thigh.

All movement ceased at the edges of the street and all eyes locked onto the looming confrontation.

"I listen only to God," Dan replied, holding the A-frame and his arched body position.

"That's kind of crazy, don't ya think?" Spivey's shadow cooled Dan's face. "After all, it seems to me your God is losing touch with society." He deliberately slanted to allow the bright rays to sting Dan's eyes into a squint. "He just slouches about in them clouds letting that old devil Lincoln run amok and take lives without any thought or reason."

"God's will is for peace to all, regardless of their politics," Dan answered, raising his palm as a sun shield and refusing to stand.

"His will ain't stopping the lead." He turned his neck to look at the gathering townsfolk. He feared Dan's words would spiritually give rise to hope and salvation.

"Peace will come." Dan decided to fully rise.

"God is blind, and the blind cannot lead the blind," Spivey mocked.

"When man seeks to love and forgive, the healing will follow," Dan quoted the Bible.

"Forgive! There'll never be any forgiving," Spivey moved closer. "Not in these parts. Never. Too many and too young have been taken from their mamas' bosoms to allow any forgiveness."

"Forgiveness is the path of the righteous," Dan said.

"Well then you'll forgive me when I tell you again that your path here has ended." Spivey expanded his chest.

"It is not your judgment to make," Dan defied.

Without further words, Spivey drew back his fist and launched it into Dan's stomach. Gasps and sniggers rose in unison as Dan folded and dropped breathless to the floor.

"Preacher with a gun!" Spivey's eyes widened. "Isn't that what Todd told us all?" he shouted. "What man of God carries a gun?"

Spivey swung a powerful kick to Dan's jaw, its accuracy stretching his neck and rolling his eyes white to blur his vision.

"What does your lord say to that?" He laughed raucously then winced as he rubbed the leather toe piece where the connection against the jaw bone had hurt his foot.

"I forgive." Dan rasped through a stream of blood.

Spivey stamped the brief pain out of his foot then he reached out to grab the sledge to flip it sidewards to tip out the wooden pieces and bark string.

Spreading the collection wide with his swinging boot he froze momentarily when he saw Dan's stretching hand reach out, however his alarm subsided when he saw the shaking fingers hook the loose bible and nip tight a curled tussle of golden hair which had blown out from the pages to dance with the dust.

Spivey spat at the lame figure and reached down to grab the pistol then throwing his head back he howled loudly.

"I am thirsty said Jesus!" Then opening his arms wide to the sky he turned to walk in the direction of the Wild Hawk.

Dan rose to one knee and wiped away the blood from his lips with his forearm. Through blurred vision he watched Spivey disappear inside the saloon then he paused to steady himself as the amused onlookers turned away with scolding mutterings to go about their daily business.

Steadying his shaky legs, he drew several shallow relieving breaths, shook his vision clear, and clenched his teeth to oust the pain and withhold angry cusses, then finally erect and composed and no longer an interest to the loiterers, undeterred from his mission he reassembled and restocked the 'A' frame to drag the wood and vines inside the church.

Stalling with surprise at the doorway his eyes dropped upon another basket of food and water which were placed in the same location as the prior night's supplies.

Although nausea had displaced his hunger, he clasped his hand tight, closed his eyes, and thanked the Lord for the offering, knowing whoever made this sacrifice was risking expulsion and persecution from their neighbour's.

He lifted the linen basket cover and joyed at the sight of cornbread, berries, boiled roots, pork tallow, and fresh water.

Then he sat in contemplation, listening to the wind rattling against unstable doors until his vigor and spirit rekindled.

After stacking his haul of materials away from prying eyes, Dan spent the rest of the day making rudimentary repairs to the church. No further incidents occurred and Dan did not venture beyond the boundary of the repaired double door.

The following day, Dan repeated his actions. Dragging the travois, he left South Cave before sun up and scoured through the debris of the ruined dwellings that prior to the war were flourishing cattle yards and homesteads.

His only deviation from the previous day's routine was that he returned to the church whilst the town was still mainly at rest, whilst only the roosters were active. Again he welcomed the sight of another restocked hamper and again he paused to thank the Lord for the necessitous deliverance. By the time the sun had drifted from the east and plunged in the west, Dan's initial repair work was mostly complete.

The roof and walls had been patched to seal out the blustery elements. A crude alter had been erected and the doors strengthened so they could be easily opened and closed. Concluding it was impossible to refit pews, he jointed several crates and used smashed boards to create a small pulpit.

Dan's final acts was to reconstruct a sturdy stairwell and position it for all to see against the now sturdy and inviting doors, then he re-secured the neglected crucifix to confirm God was on duty.

Satisfied with his work, he sat in the darkness pondering how he would attract an audience for Sunday worship whilst Spivey and his cronies domineered the townsfolk and hindered them from attending any religious observance with the new pastor from across the water.

He knew in the absence of conscripted males there was no one of sufficient strength or courage to challenge the intimidators.

He grappled with his anger and struggled to hold it back. For a brief moment he considered matching violence with violence and he recited a phrase from Exodus 'An eye for an eye and a tooth for a tooth' but then he shook away the temptation and replaced the quote with the words of Matthew 'If anyone slaps you on the right cheek, turn to him the other also.'

He slumped in a corner and resting his back against the timber he pulled his knees up to his chest. Throughout the night he tortured himself, he knew he could equal Spivey's brutality with his own fierceness, but his loyalty to God admonished his sinful thoughts and he replaced them with the words of the Romans 'Never avenge yourself, leave it to the wrath of God.'

He continued his deliberation feeling despondent until the creaking of door opening alerted him. Twisting his head in the direction of the danger, moon glow briefly flooded the inside of the church with its luster allowing Dan to make out within the silver flash the figure of a slender woman.

"Can I help you?" He called out calmly from the dark corner.

The silhouette figure stopped in the frame of the doorway.

"Hello." Dan arose and took a few slow steps toward the static figure then stopped where he too could be seen in the moonlight. "Can I help you?" He noticed the woman who was shocked by his presence, paused and remained silent. He saw she was cradling a basket. "Do not be afraid. I mean you no harm." He held up the flat of both of his hands to express his sincerity. She remained ridged.

"I'm sorry. I thought you were at the watering hole." She said softly, with a nervous tremor.

Her words were almost inaudible to Dan's ears. "Sorry."

"The Wild Hawk." She clarified quietly. "That's where all the men go to cure their thirst. I mean, that's where they hung out before the war called them."

"Ah, I see." He took a timed step in her direction. "Well, apparently I'm not welcome."

"I did wonder." In the faint light, he saw her flurry her brow and begin to study him, but suddenly the peaceful and polite preliminaries were interrupted by shouting and cursing beyond the door.

"Killer you in there!"

Both Dan and the woman angled their heads toward the door, she released a nervous gasp.

"I know you're in there, you traitorous son of a bitch."

Dan silently stepped forward to peek through a gap in the wall panels and the woman held her palm over her mouth to prevent her from screaming.

"I heard voices so I know you're in there."

He saw in the center of the street Flint Spivey staggering towards the church steps. In his right hand he was waving his pistol above his head and in his left, he gripped tight a bottle.

Illumination suddenly flared as a blast of lead was fired skywards. The woman screamed and dropped the basket to the floor.

Her eyes round and bulging with fear she looked at Dan for protection.

"Who you got in there, you cowardly son of a bitch!"

Dan saw Spivey level the wavering pistol towards the church door, instinctively he leaped forward wrapping his arms around the woman, and using his body as a shield he shunted her back a few steps just as another bullet thudded into the wood.

"Get out here you Yankee son of a whore!" Another bullet tore a hole through a thin timber slat and splinters showered the floor.

Reaching out to slam the door shut, Dan gently guided the woman toward the corner of the building for protection.

As he silently urged her down to her knees the intermittent sprays of moonlight shone on her face and he was surprised to notice the innocence of her youth. She noticed his eyes narrow with astonishment, but quickly and almost embarrassingly, he turned away and furtively gazed around the church as if he were searching for something.

"What are you doing?"

"I can reason with him." He replied.

"No. Please you can't go out there." She shook her head and stood as if to block his way. "There is no reasoning with him."

"Please stay here." He asked calmly, but it was implied as a demand which she understood.

"He won't come in here."

"I'm unarmed, and he knows that. He will not shoot."

"He won't care." Panic trembled through her. "You can't go out there he'll kill you."

Dan placed his hands on the girl's shoulders and he began to ease her to his side, but another two shots pierced more holes in the door and instantly forced them both to cower low.

Dan reached out and dragged a crate behind the girl to act as a shield.

"God will protect me." He did not believe his faith could stop the thunder of lead, but he needed to reassure the girl.

"As he did my father?"

Dan did not need to ask. The grief in her eyes told him she was one of the many who grieved in this county.

"Get out here preach. I've got a message for you."

Dan tried to recall the number of shots fired as he straightened himself.

"Go home Flint!" An anonymous call bellowed out from a distant cabin.

"Mind your own darn business!" Spivey slurred over his shoulder. "I've got a message for God."

More calls were raised from the darkness, calling for Spivey to quit and go home to bed. He spun, waving his pistol aimlessly into the dark. "Shut it all of ya. I do the calling round here."

Dan moved to peek through the gap to the door to watch the nuisance swaying on his feet with his gun wildly swinging above his head as he shouted out to the cowardly hecklers who dared not show beyond the cabin doors and windows.

Suddenly Spivey fired off another shot which splintered just above Dan's head causing him again to shudder and duck low

Silence fell until Dan pulled back the door to reveal himself.

"Son of a bitch." Slowly Spivey noticed the ghost like figure standing high on the repaired steps. Poisoned by whiskey, he struggled to hold his legs firm beneath him as he gawked upwards.

"I've got a message for God." He slurred. "And I want you to deliver it ... in person."

"Service is at ten. You're more than welcome."

"You ain't listening Yank."

"Flint! Flint!" Shouted a rushing woman who appeared from the obscurity. "Just what do you think you are doing this time of night?"

"None of your God darn business." He held out the flat of his hand to dismiss her.

"Get yourself home before you wake up the whole town."

"They need to wake up and open their eyes to see what's going on here with this northern devil."

She knocked away his outstretched arm and grabbed his elbow.

"God darn Yankee traitor come to gloat." He pointed with the barrel of the pistol and at the same time he pulled on the trigger again. The bullet hissed to the side of Dan's head and it thudded into the wood next to him.

Wobbling, Spivey shook away the woman's grip, then he used his forearm to push her away and as she staggered backward he flipped open his pistol to attempt reloading. He fumbled with the lead in his fingers and he dropped the bullets to the floor when the angered woman charged forward again with a determination to take a firmer grip. In no stable condition to oppose her fury, Spivey released an onslaught of cusses at his wife, the Lord, the devil, the preacher, and Lincoln as he was dragged away from the center of the street.

The woman flicked a scowl in Dan's direction and he sensed her intervention was not for his benefit and that she was not his savior.

Dan watched Spivey stagger away with zigzag steps and the stiff brace of his annoyed wife. Waving a balled fist at the church his slurred cussing continued as his silhouetted figure diminished into the dark and his anger became inaudible.

Turning to enter the church, Dan shook his head and, using the fold of his fingers, he again counted the gunshots.

"Where there is drink, there is danger." He said, shaking his head knowing he had miscounted.

"That's Flint Spivey." The girl announced. She had moved out from behind the protection of the crate to watch the conclusion of the affair over Dan's shoulder. "And his wife Helen."

"I've had the pleasure." He closed the door. "You're the one who has been bringing me the food." He smiled.

"You seem surprised."

"Surprised by your courage. Especially for one so young."

He could not see her blush. "I'm not that young." She seemed to rise a few inches.

"I admit." Dan pressed the flat of his palms together. "Whilst I may be surprised I am grateful for your help. I did not anticipate nor plan for such a hostile greeting and without your blessings, I would have starved."

"Yeah, some folks are pretty mean around here." She bent her knees and lowered, but keeping her back straight, she held her gaze at the pastor as she gathered and reassembled the food in the basket.

"That so." Aware of her scrutiny he turned and feigned an inspection of the bullet damage.

"It's true. Especially Spivey and Dandy. They are out to just bully and scare everybody into doing just what they want and when they want it."

"I figured."

Dan did not finish, the girl cut in talking nervously fast, and without breath, she found it necessary to continue.

"Dandy owns most of the land around these parts and he rents out cabins and homesteads to us normal folk. In fact, he owns just about every building except the Wild Hawk and this old church."

"Something kind of makes sense now." Dan briefly reflected on his experience within the saloon.

"He's always threatening to evict folk if they don't follow his command. Dandy is the brains and Spivey is his brawn." She rose up the basket and stretched out her arm to hand the food to Dan. "Dandy is pure evil and Spivey, well just does what he is told. He's kind of dumb."

He nodded and smiled to accept the offering. "Dandy?" He baited.

"He's the little rattler with the glasses. Tyree Dandridge, but we call him Dandy. Only thing is dandy, he ain't." Her eyes widened to emphasise her warning. "He's as cold as ice who takes to killing easy."

"And that's why no one will come to prayers."

"Most likely. With all the men away fighting, there's no one left here who dare oppose them."

"And Spivey? Why is he so?" Dan did not add the final word, his frown confirmed what he was thinking. "Is it because I came in from over the river."

"He is a bitter man." She said quietly, with a concerning shake of her head. "You see he's lost family in this war. His son Abe ran away to fight as the war broke, but he was reported dead at Deer Springs. Spivey went out there to bring him home, but all he came back with was his cap and a few letters."

Dan lit a candle which he found in the basket as he listened. The weak hue confirmed the youthfulness of the girl. Out of politeness and to avoid embarrassing the girl Dan did not study her features and after noting her hair was concealed behind a bonnet and she was wrapped in an oversized shawl, he averted his eyes to the contents of the basket.

"Poor Helen, I mean Mrs Spivey. She's gone darn near crazy ever since trying to control his meanness. She's rarely seen outside her cabin and she doesn't talk to no one anymore. They both took it really hard b'cos he was their only boy."

"The kepi is the boys." He looked up from the food.

"Never takes it off."

"He didn't go fight?" Dan wondered.

"He led the local militia until they fled when the Yankees came. They all scat and he did too, but since he came back there ain't been any men left in town he can call upon."

"And you? Why are you taking such risks?" He asked.

"We are not all like Dandy and Spivey. There are many of us who have loved ones who are away fighting and we need a disciple of God to hear our prayers. We pray every night at home, but my mama say's there is no place more powerful for giving belief and hope than from the inside of a church."

"Your mama sent you with the food?"

"Doesn't the bible say 'whoever shuts their eyes and ears to the needs of the hungry will not have their prayers answered."

"Not quite." Dan smiled, explaining God wants to help everyone. He offered her some bread and dried fruit which she declined and they talked for some time.

He learned she was called Isabella Lister, although she liked to be known as Issy. She was only sixteen and both her older brother Rudy and her father Isaac left home two years ago to join up with the army of Tennessee.

Issy worried that she had received only one letter from her Pa many months ago and now she feared the worst as most of the townsfolk had been gossiping that the army of Tennessee had been bushwhacked up near Stones River. Since then Issy, her mama and a war orphan 'Ray' whom they adopted had suffered injustices just as many other locals had due to the hardships of war and the unforeseen circumstances which left them at the mercy of Dandridge and Spivey.

Dan talked about his mission in South Cave and explained to Issy his calling. In return, she listened excitedly to his expressive passions, belief's and objectives.

Noting it was getting late and seeing her eyelids blink heavily, he offered to walk her home, however she refused, insisting that she only lived 'a stone's throw away' from the church.

Promising to return with more pack ups and to attend his next service, with a chilly shudder under her evening wrap she excitedly sped towards her cabin eager to inform her mama of her new found knowledge.

Parting at the door he thanked her again for the food and he watched her skip away to the welcome of her mother's shadow.

Dan kept a watchful eye on the girl until she disappeared into the darkness then darting a glance to the scattering of flickering stars he thanked the Lord for confirming he was needed in South Cave.

Chapter 6

The next two days passed without any violence, and on the fourth day, accompanied by wide-eyed children's gazes, Dan hung a large cross on the door. Then he scratched a notice deep into the flaky white paint of the main door: *'Services Every Sunday at 10 and Wednesday at dark.'*

Spivey and Dandridge continued to harass with passing threats and scornful tirades regarding nonattendance and participation, whilst the rest of the town's occupants gawked on from a distance with fearful curiosity and no commitment.

Issy continued to bravely provide regular baskets of food, and on one windswept afternoon it appeared to Dan that her mother, Jemima, intended to pay him a visit, but noticing Dandridge scowling towards her approach as he leant on a hitch rail opposite, she spun on her heels and disappeared. At dark on Wednesday, only Issy attended the first service. Clutching a handful of candles, a bunch of wildflowers, and her Bible, she defied the peeping and the unwilling who watched on from behind their curtains and cracked doors, and she marched with her neck high and her face fixed ahead to pray for peace, love, and the return of her father and brother.

Undeterred by his immediate lack of appeal to the residents, Dan determinedly carried on, and from on high, using the crates, he delivered a service calling for faith and compassion to his only worshipper.

However, inwardly he was upset by the lack of exchange, not just by Dandridge's and Spivey's overbearing presence, but by the townsfolk's apprehensive and passive acceptance of their humiliation.

Upon the closure of the singing and recitals, Issy jubilantly strode home, ignoring the silent gauntlet of suspicious glares. A buoyancy of newfound spirit had been injected into her mind, and invigorated fresh beliefs of hope radiated in her beaming clear eyes. Dan looked out from the steps, bold and brave. He expected retaliatory repercussions from South Cave's aggressors, but only swirling dirt gathered on the street as he watched Issy embrace a welcoming and relieved hug at the entrance of her home. Closing the door behind her, Jemima cast a benevolent smile in the direction of the pastor, and he returned the subtlest of nods as he too disappeared behind the closing doors.

Dan laboured hard again during the next couple of days.

He burnt wild bush and debris which he had cleared from around the church, and after gathering more scraps and crates, he managed to shape four benches which he positioned to act as pews.

Several times he endured insults and threats, and at one point a small gathering warned they were going to claim the wood and use it for his own funeral pyre.

Ignoring their threats of viciousness, he stood firm and recited Jeremiah's and Luke's forgiveness: 'For I will forgive their wickedness and I will remember their sins no more.' 'Do not judge and you shall not be judged. Do not condemn and you shall not be condemned. Forgive and you shall be forgiven.'

Without Dandridge or Spivey to bolster their bravery, the crowd soon dissipated with discontented grumbles calling for the Yank to be run out of town.

Issy again attended the next service alone, but at the Wednesday service she was accompanied by her nervous-looking mother, and the following Sunday the mother and daughter were joined by two elderly widows who covered their lowered heads with clean, starched bonnets.

Midway through the service, heckling from beyond the church doors penetrated the wooden repairs and interrupted the benediction. The worshippers feared the voices on the street were dissenters who were congregating beyond the closed doors, and apprehension immediately dispirited their vibrant tones.

Dan's vigour diminished, and the verses drifted to a near silence as the volume of the ruckus increased. Without displaying his inward anxiety to the females, he stepped down from the crate and marched towards the door to confront the unholy assembly.

He paused in front of the timber, drew in a large composing breath, and tucked his Bible securely in his belt.

To his surprise, he smelt the fragrant freshness of Issy and Jemima. They had left their seated positions quietly to brace either side of him whilst his senses were occupied and distracted with the looming confrontation that awaited beyond the doors.

"What is it?" Jemima asked.

"I'm not sure, but something ain't right." Dan frowned. He squinted through the slats, but the street to the front of the church was empty.

"Is it Spivey?"

"I'm not sure." The commotion continued, and Dan caught glimpses of people running past the church. "Something's not right."

"Don't go out there." Jemima placed a gentle restraining hand on his shoulder. "You know they have nothing but bad intentions."

"Someone may need God's help." He smiled a calming return to her apprehensive frown.

"You can't go. It will be dangerous." Her fear did not abate.

"I must." He nodded his intent. "For such is God's will."

He peered again quizzically through the slats at the passersby who sped towards the edge of town.

"Then we will come with you."

He met the offer with a pleasing smile, but his acceptance gave way to a sternness that jolted them. "You must not leave here. Stay inside and devote yourselves to prayers." He cracked open the door and levered his head through the gap. "I will soon return."

"We stand by your side."

Jemima's assertion surprised him, and he pulled his shoulder back within the church and closed the door.

"Then stay safe and pray."

The women noticed all the speculation in his expression had been ousted by alarm.

"You came when we called you." Issy referred to her prayers for salvation.

"This is my walk, which I must take alone."

He half turned to each of the women and nodded his gratitude, and with an accompanying benign smile he gently ushered them away from the door.

Returning to narrow his eyes and peer once more between the gaps in the slats, moments later he swung out the doors slowly to avoid attention.

At first, he stretched out from the top of the steps with his frame to view the angry crowd at the far end of the street, and for a moment he watched a tirade of protestations and angry arm-waving. Then he stepped down from the newly repaired steps to tread amongst the vehement crowd to investigate the sudden upheaval.

As he neared the crowd, his face twisted with confusion when, to his dismay, he saw the gathering horde was not rallying to hurl their abuse towards the church, but with their backs towards him the townsfolk were engaged in another sinister protestation.

Through the barrier of bodies, he could hear disdain, cusses, and expletive language being raged in unison. Carefully, Dan elbowed his way through the shoulders until the target of their abuse distressed his eyes.

Bound by the wrists to a horse and being dragged along the street was a blue-clad captive. In the midst of his adolescence, the youth was screaming out for help and mercy. His blonde hair was stained red with blood, and the centre of his forehead displayed a plum-sized purple swelling.

Pleading to all around him, tears streaked the side of his dirt-covered face, and blood seeped from the tight binding around his wrists. The boy struggled to remain upright, and he fell numerous times to his bone-raw knees. Unperturbed by the distress of his captive, the rider continued to urge on his horse along Main Street to parade his prisoner to the raucous crowd, with drips of blood parallel to the hoof prints identifying the harrowing route from the distant hill to the centre of the town.

"Look what we got ourselves, fellas!" shouted the rider, waving his hat in one hand to the crowd with an unbridled celebratory boast to equal his triumphant joy. "Caught the weasel sneaking about in Old Hazel Woods."

Drawing to a halt alongside the main bulk of cheers and whoopee calls, the man dismounted and hauled the exhausted boy to his feet.

"What in darnation shall we do with him?" said a woman, stepping up to the boy and pulling his hair to raise his head.

The crowd parted. "What we ain't going to do is spank his butt and send him back home to his mama." Dandridge emerged to stand in front of the boy. "Hell no."

The woman released the boy's blood-matted hair and spat on the back of his sagging head.

"He'd hightail it straight back over yonder to the blue bellies and bring 'em right back here." Spivey stepped down from the boardwalk to tread Dandridge's path. "And we ain't allowing that. Are we now, folks?"

He flicked his eyes around the semi-circle of spectators, who all returned satanic sneers and head shakes.

"We need to find out where the rest of them are hauled up. See if there is something we ought to be doing." Bill Todd footed the steps from the boardwalk.

"Pump him until he squeals out where the rest of them are hauled up!" Spivey shouted.

Dandridge leaned over and, along with the abductor, hauled the boy to his feet. Exhausted and nearing unconsciousness, the boy's legs would not hold him upright, and he was prevented from a full collapse by the man who held him firm by wrapping his arms under the boy's armpits and clamping them around his chest.

"Well, one thing is for certain." Dandridge said, squeezing the boy's cheeks between his fingers and thumb. "We can't let him go."

"You must!" Dan stepped out from between the heaving bodies, his right hand pressing his Bible tight against his chest. "He can stay with me in the church until it is safe for his release."

"This young fella is not a fighting man." Dan had seen the boy's broken drumsticks tucked within his belt. "He is a musician. A drummer whose only task is to keep up the spirits of his kin."

"You keep out of this, Yank!"

"None of your God-darn business."

"He would say that."

"Protecting his own."

Numerous other insults were spat all at once, but Dan's attention was focused on the condition of the boy, and his ears did not acknowledge the words of hate.

"We know your colour, preacher, and we know you play the devil's fiddle," dismissed Dandridge.

"I just want to go home, sir," the boy rasped quietly, his throat parched with dust, his blood-veined eyes angled towards the clergyman.

"Hold your God-darn tongue." Dandridge firmed his grip on the boy's face.

"And shut your God-forsaken shithole." Spivey thrust forward to deliver a powerful chopping kick against the boy's thigh. "You're going nowhere but to the dirt."

The boy's legs gave way, but the grip of his capturer held him upright.

Dandridge released the boy's face and turned square to the preacher.

Dan met the fierce glare. "The boy is no threat. He is just a drum player."

"He beats to the devil's march," Dandridge condemned.

"No harm must come to him." Dan turned to appeal to the barbarous throng. "He is an innocent child of God."

"God is with us."

"He fights against the devils from the north."

"God has delivered him unto us."

Their calls of castigation pierced deep into Dan's heart, but he would not relent, and holding his Bible high, he appealed, "The only enemy here is death."

The venomous abuse and threats raged on from all sides. Dan darted hopelessly between the protagonists, pleading for them to exonerate the boy for his ignorance. He shook them one after another rapidly by the shoulders with desperation, knowing the boy's life was in peril.

He glimpsed from a distance the hopeless look in Jemima's eyes, and he despaired when he saw her urge him to admit defeat and leave the boy to the slaughter when she shook her head and lowered her face.

"Hang the son of a bitch!"

"Make him squeal."

"Torture him!"

"We need to know where the rest of the heathens are hiding."

"Stretch his neck."

"Take him to the hanging tree."

"Rope him up."

"No! No! No!" Dan's command could not be heard above the hate and all-round cheers and calls for vengeance.

"Stop this senselessness! Listen to you all. He is just a boy!" Dan recoiled from one angry face to another until he collided with Dandridge.

"Listen to me!" He grabbed Dandridge by the collar with one hand and held the Bible up to Dandridge's face. "No harm must come to this boy."

"He chose to follow the path of Satan, but God has led him unto us." Dandridge pushed away the Bible and pulled back to break from the hold. "If we let him return to the lair of the devil, Satan himself will unleash his fury upon this town."

"Nonsense. This boy is like one of your own … look at him … look at him … he needs help."

Still held upright, the drummer boy's head sagged limp and tears wetted his shirt as he incessantly mumbled delirious cries for help.

"None of our boys have ever returned home!" shouted a woman whose dark attire denoted her mourning.

Rapturous cheers and calls of support infected the air.

"To the tree!" the unforgiving crowd began to chant.

The boy gasped and released a terrified shriek.

"Stop now. Look at you all." Dan tucked his Bible in his belt and leaped to wrap his arm around the boy to protect him. "Thirsty for the murder of a young boy." He tried to wrestle the boy from the hold of the abductor. "What's become of you all?"

"War and death!" screamed the woman in black.

"The slaughter of our loved ones by the blue devils," shouted someone next to her.

"Do not avenge evil with evil," Dan begged as he struggled to break the boy free.

"One more word from you, heathen, and you'll be swinging next to him."

Dan felt the cold steel of Spivey's pistol press against his temple. He knew only the white collar would not protect him from execution, and he eased back from the struggle.

"Hang them both," Dandridge ordered.

The boy's eyes dilated, and he released a petrified sigh. Dan's heart thumped uncontrollably, and he suddenly became breathless.

The crowd surged forward as one to reach and grasp at Dan, but he lunged forward again to pull the boy tight against his body and clasped his arms around his shoulders. He held him tight and braced himself as angry claws scratched, grabbed, and pulled him violently.

Spivey was hurled sidewards, and he stumbled to the feet of the onrushers.

Still, Dan held firm and, closing his eyes, recited forgiveness from the verse of Daniel as limbs pulled him in all directions.

Dandridge's patience had expired, and he launched himself high above the heads of the aggressors to swing his pistol and crack its steel hard against the side of Dan's unprotected head. Instantly, Dan's legs betrayed him and his vision spun uncontrollably as he thudded to the floor.

Instinctively, he tried to wrap his arms tight around the boy's legs, but trampling feet and repeated kicks soon weakened his grasp.

His last blurry vision was of the screaming boy and the furrows left in the soil by his dragged feet. Dan did not feel the second pistol-whipping, nor the third or the fourth.

Chapter 7

At first, the inaudible comments failed to register in his ears as pain and crippling palpitations clasped his entire body. Dan felt a damp cloth gently swathe his forehead. He tried to hold up his hand to the dim light that penetrated through his closed eyelids, but an all-consuming raging fire of misery and pain ravaged his every nerve and fibre, and so he began to willingly allow the blackness of sleep to relieve his impelling affliction and lure him back into unconsciousness.

Jemima and Issy continued to apply cold damp cloths to his burning forehead, and they dappled water onto his swollen lips. Homemade tinctures, compresses, and herbal remedies were constant throughout the remainder of the day and the entire night as the Listers tended to Dan's wounds and presided over his convalescence.

Gradually he became aware of the presence of the helpers, and he suspected from their voices, which were almost lost in an indistinguishable hum, that they were Issy and Jemima. He tried to respond by opening his mouth and accepting the water they offered, but still, paralysing bouts of pain held him both mute and motionless.

He could not smell their usual freshness or fill his lungs with a burst of cool invigoration because rank, dried blood blocked his nostrils.

He fought against the agony again to flicker an eyelid and speak, but contortions of unbearable pain gouged at his temples, forcing him to hold tight both his mouth and eyelids as the pain intruded.

With great effort, he raised his head and chest, using his elbows as leverage. Jemima cradled his bulk, and Issy managed to ladle more droplets of water into his mouth. He groaned as the earlier events flooded back, and he momentarily forgot about the pain as his mind anguished over the baneful incident.

"They didn't," he rasped, opening one eye just enough to register the women's upset faces confirming the boy was hanged.

"You must rest," Jemima said, gazing at his swollen and bruised face.

He knew she was right and, unable to respond, his body sagged and he eased back into slumber.

Two sun-ups passed before Dan was able to stand unassisted.

His injuries were not healed; however, his stomach had been filled with Jemima's hot broil and he was strong enough to walk unaided.

He dragged his aching joints to the door and cracked it open just enough to see the boy still swinging from the hanging tree.

The low morning sun cast a long shadow far across the street from the imposing trunk with its thick branches and the boy with no name.

Dan's stomach rolled. He lowered his shaking head, then turned to face the two animated women.

They instinctively knew his next actions, and they looked at each other, wondering how they could stop him.

"There will be a mama somewhere left for all eternity wondering where her boy is and why he never returned home." Although weakened and still in discomfort, the execution had not sapped his vigour. The cold-blooded murderers sickened him, and he refused to accept their evil.

"You can't." Jemima warned him to stay within the safety of the church.

"I need to see if he has any papers," he announced his intentions.

"It's not safe."

"He needs a blessing and a place to lie."

"If you walk through those doors you must leave this place for good. It's not safe for you here. You've seen how they behave."

"I do not fear them." Dan's eyes narrowed as though he was searching for something. "And my work here is not yet done."

"Your faith is misjudged." Jemima stepped to his front to block his roaming vision.

"God's presence must stop them, and it will stop the evildoers." Their eyes collided.

"It was me that saved you from the noose, not God." Jemima held the stare, hoping for a reaction. "And I fear I will not be able to do it again."

Dan tilted his head as if he was going to say something, but instead, he angled himself past her static stance without a reply.

"If they'll hang a boy in cold blood, do you think their remorse will protect you?"

He stamped on a crate until he held up a dagger-shaped piece of wood.

"I will not abandon his soul to Hades."

Jemima sighed and looked at Issy. She returned a nod, signalling Jemima to grab the muslin sack.

"Here, take these." Rising to meet Dan's curious look, she held out the sack. "These were my husband's." She walked near to Dan and pushed the weighty bag against his chest, then released it into his reactive grasp.

"He fought and killed men with these?" Dan asked as he opened the sack to his eyes.

"They have seen death, and you need protection. This is why I'm giving them to you," she replied.

"Neither your book nor your prayers will save you out there," Issy worried.

Without touching them, Dan inspected the tarnished aged Colt Dragoon pistol, a rusty boot knife, and the dozen or so bullets.

"Isaac left me these for protection."

He doubted the working capability of the gun, and the knife was blunt.

His lips remained together and, lifting out the knife, he then closed the bag and lifted it in her direction.

She anticipated his reaction. "If a situation arose, I ain't steady enough to use a gun, so it ain't any use to me."

"Thank you, but I don't need it."

"Then I pity you. Things being what they are here, I fear for you." A noticeable quiver trembled in her voice.

"I thank you for your concern and—"

Jemima cut him off mid-sentence. "You may preach and holler to the Lord for forgiveness for what they have done, but in your fever I heard you promise retribution."

"I was delirious." He shook his head to dismiss her claim.

"I can see it in your eyes." She moved close so that her face was near his. "Your heart burns for vengeance."

"I did not know what I was saying."

"Your soul has spoken. Your words were true."

Dan turned away, silently shaking his head.

"You cannot deny your conscience." She persisted, hoping her reminiscence would make him change his mind and take the gun for protection.

"I can't leave the boy to the peckers. He deserves better."

Securing the knife in his belt, Dan pulled open the door and glanced north and south along the street, but as usual there was no activity and the boardwalks were empty.

Before he closed the door behind him, he looked over his shoulder and for a moment he held a stare as Jemima forlornly wrapped her arms around her daughter. They both knew he was beyond saving and they expected the next time they saw him, they would be looking at a corpse.

With a heave, he broke the early morning stillness by dragging his sledge toward the hanging tree.

He paused at the small bare feet of the dead boy to look up at the pained and twisted ashen face. Glassy eyes half-closed and drool hanging from a bitten tongue, the boy's death grimace was one of pure terror and not one of peace, as was his right.

Drawing in a deep suppressing breath, Dan reached low to pick up the fallen drumsticks, then he cupped the boy's cold hand in his palm and said a brief prayer. Tucking the wooden rods into his belt, he positioned the 'A' frame so that he could stretch high with the knife to cut the rope. However, unable to catch the boy's fall with his free hand, the body fell with a sickening crunch and Dan closed his eyes as a quiver sped along his spine. About him he felt the glares from the curtain twitches, but again scanning the empty street he saw and heard no one.

The day was still young, and the lack of hostility indicated to him the troublemakers were almost certainly still sleeping off last night's poisoned excesses.

Unconcerned for his own safety, he respectfully turned the boy onto the frame and searched inside his jacket without success for identification. Despondent and exhausted, he rested on one knee a while before dragging the body up the slope in the direction of the cemetery.

By noon the task was complete. He had chiselled out a shallow grave, laid the boy to rest with a deep covering of dirt, and erected a marker in the shape of a cross with the carved tribute: *'Here lays one of God's children.'*

Then with his head hung low, exhausted and thirsty, he dragged the 'A' frame back along Main Street.

"I don't know if you're brave, plain stupid, or both." Dandridge leaned on the side rail looking at the preacher's raw and bleeding callouses.

"Couldn't just leave him swinging."

Dan gritted his teeth and silently called out to God to help him control his inner beliefs, show restraint, and prevent an angered retaliation.

"Sure you could." Dandridge smiled.

"Once the buzzards had eaten their fill, he'd eventually drop to the prairie dogs and rats."

"It's unholy and unlawful what you've done to that boy."

"If I were you, I wouldn't worry too much about that." Dandridge spat into his kerchief. "I'd be thinking about my own self-preservation right now, and I'd be doing it real quick."

"One day you will feel God's wrath," Dan hoped.

"You think?"

"God watches all."

"Well, I sure hope he keeps a safe eye out for you." Dandridge removed his glasses and began to clean them as he intimidated.

"The Lord guides me. I do not worry and I do not need your advice."

Dan heard a door pull ajar behind him. He glanced over his shoulder to glimpse an obscured onlooker. He then noticed the usual curtains twitching and several dawdlers gathering at a safe distance. Mutterings of disbelief and condemnation for what he had done began to rise in volume, and the preacher was downhearted by their disapproval.

"And fools don't take it." Dandridge smiled, carefully replacing the eyewear.

"A fool thinks himself to be wise," Dan replied with a gutsy smile. "But a wise man knows himself to be a fool."

"Why damn you, preacher." Dandridge returned the smile and straightened himself, then moved towards the boardwalk steps. "For you must be one of a kind."

He laughed and tapped his fingers menacingly against the handle of his pistol. "There'll be no more warnings coming your way, preach," he threatened. "You hear me!"

The loudness of his prophecy increased as, irritatingly, he saw the preacher had the gall to turn his back on him and walk towards the well. "Stay here and you'll end up being planted next to that boy!"

Dan contained his anger and walked away from the impelling confrontation. He saw disappointed frowns, and he heard the disgruntled moans from the bystanders who hoped to see more violence and the bloodshed of another Yank.

Before drawing the pail from the well, he feathered his fingers across his raw callouses. Dismissing the soreness, he considered the pain a small but worthy necessity he must suffer for delivering the soul of the boy to God. He plunged his stinging hands into the coolness of the water and held them in deep for a few moments to allow the burning to ease and then, throwing away the tainted water, he refilled the pail with a fresh supply to scoop into the dipper. The cold ladle had just touched his dry lips when a swinging fist knocked the scoop skywards and splashed water in all directions.

"Like an annoying flea that's not welcome." Spivey had been watching the conversation from the comfort of his porch rocker, and the preacher's boldness had irked him into malice.

He pushed Dan hard on the chest to force him away from the well.

"Take heed of my friend's advice and get out of our town."

Dan was unbalanced, and he staggered a few steps until eventually he fell. Spivey hung his clawed hand next to his pistol and sneered at the man's weakness.

"Whilst you're still able to stand."

Dan's lips remained tight and, to Spivey's annoyance, he did not commit to a response. Instead, he simply wiped the water from his face and the dust from his clothes, then, holding a defiant stare just long enough to see Spivey's eyes narrow and the veins on his temples bulge, he turned his back on the aggressor.

Ignoring the tirade of threats, insults, and mocks, he returned to the dim coolness of the church.

"The sun's going down on you, preach!" was the last threat to reach Dan's ears as he closed the church door to block out the noon brightness.

Inside the false serenity, Dan sighed. He rested for a moment with his back against the door and gritted his teeth.

Determinedly he confirmed to himself he would not allow disenchanting thoughts or fear of the gun-wielding bullies to taint God's mission.

Jemima and Issy had returned home, he hoped, leaving behind their remedies, some food, and the pistol. He shook his head, knowing there was no place for a life-taker in the house of God.

The rest of the day crawled into dusk without further incidents or adversity for Dan.

Troubled by the soreness of his hands, he refrained from any arduous labour, choosing instead to use the brilliance of the light shards that splintered the wall panels to read the letters of the holy scriptures until his eyes and thoughts needed rest.

Chapter 8

As darkness enveloped the town, undeterred by the oppressing nihilists, Dan swung open the church doors wide and fastened them secure, hoping to offer welcoming greetings for those who braved the evening service.

As he hoped, Jemima and Issy defied the few inquisitive gatherers to climb the four door steps and accept the kindly smile of the preacher. In their hands they carried a basket of fresh nourishment and more homemade remedies created to ease Dan's sores and bruises. To his surprise, following on behind to join them were Issy, the orphan Ray, and the two old widows linked arm in arm with a one-legged war veteran.

Instead of closing the doors to perform his sermon, Dan broke from tradition to allow his prayers, verses, and hymns to penetrate the usual tranquillity that descended with the accompanying darkness.

Raising his eyes from his scripture, Dan noticed a straggle of fleeting faces appear at the entrance, mainly aged females, but after a few moments of hesitation their nerves failed them and they moved on again to despair in the darkness.

Dan allowed himself a smile, and he continued his recitals with energy, knowing his work had begun to arouse the attention of the deprived followers of God.

After completion of the service, Jemima stayed behind and fixed a poultice for his scabbing callouses whilst he feasted on cornbread and preserved vegetables.

Tending to his wounds, she explained most of what he already knew with one astonishing confession. She told how the town had been ravaged many times by skirmishers from both the armies of the North and the South, and the locals had been left near starving and desperate for food.

Sympathetically, he listened to her words explaining the citizens had few commodities or supplies and so they had to be selfish to ensure their own self-preservation and endurance.

There was no help or sympathy from anyone for any of the war-scarred folk of South Cave. Meanness and suspicion brooded everywhere, and it wasn't long before resentment and animosity greeted all who dared to grace the boardwalks.

He learned that after her husband left home to volunteer for the fight, at first she managed to put food on the table by working at the school, but it wasn't long before the school was sacrificed and closed due to the war and, as a result, she needed to sell off all of her valuables and treasures to survive.

He was not surprised when her eyes welled and her account troubled him, but in her tears he could not help but notice there was not only an appealing softness in her appearance, but a graceful warmth that beautified her shyness he had not seen until now.

She seemed shy of affection, yet to Dan she possessed a rare type of beauty, one that shone from her soul. It was the first time he had noticed her qualities, and now the allure of her flesh held his gaze for too long. Even though it was the look of an honest soul, he felt embarrassed and ashamed. He diverted his eyes, hoping she had not noticed his overlong appreciation.

"Both the South and North have sacrificed in this tide of slaughter and there are many wives and mothers who have suffered the same pain and lamentations as I, but I have been forced to sin to survive." She sobbed into her hands and lowered her head, unaware of the holy man's emotions.

"Only one man offered me and Issy any help and assistance, and his advance was not welcome."

Dan did not interrupt. Instead, he just cautiously returned his compassionate gaze as he listened.

"Tyree Dandridge made it more than obvious he was in search of a wife, and it was his opinion that he and I should be blessed by uniting in marriage."

She paused several times to wipe her cheek and draw composing gasps. "He insisted that I was a widow and he was unrelenting in his pursuit of companionship."

She explained how he tried to convince her that he offered salvation from misery and that a better life awaited her and the girl if they united as man and wife.

He would not concede to the continual rejections and, as his harassment intensified, he began to intimidate anyone whom he thought may hinder his endeavours. As her hardship and desperation increased, his intentions intensified, and rather than dismiss his delusions, she kept the harmony by accepting offerings of supplies for feigned fondness.

Although staying loyal and faithful to her husband, the sin and guilt of accepting his inducements tormented her, and she asked the pastor to help her pray for forgiveness.

"Our heart does not always agree with our behaviour. You are neither a sinner nor a charlatan, although the danger you face will not yield."

He consoled her, taking hold of her wet palm and encouraging her to continue. She made it clear that she would remain resolute and never stand under a floral arch, dressed in white to honour and obey such a beast as Dandridge, no matter how tough times became.

However, she admitted to Dan that she did not know how to end the misery.

Unable to prevent herself from a self-imposed chastening, her cheeks flushed, but in the semi-darkness Dan did not notice. She hated Dandridge, and her opinion of him and his cronies was that they were the dregs of those who had been left behind whilst all men of strength and honour marched with pride at the side of Bobby Lee.

Dan commented that the problem of Dandridge would not go away by shutting it away in the dark, but God would show salvation if she remained loyal to her beliefs and slowly and carefully severed herself from Dandridge's immoral shadow.

As the hours passed, Jemima learned of his exploits and she pitied the pastor for his own sufferings. Underneath his tough exterior and pained features his eyes bore evidence of trust, warmth, and friendship.

He had the presence of a man who possessed great humanity which had been developed, softened, and denoted by tragedy, yet his vulnerabilities had only been resolved by faith.

By the end of the evening, a mutual bond formed that was beyond any religious convictions, and as Jemima stepped away into the stillness of the night Dan began to wonder if he had allowed his feelings to transgress the realms of religion.

Four days later he made the same preparations for his next service, and he was not surprised when Jemima and Issy, the widows, and the veteran were joined on the crates by another two females and an old-timer with a long white beard to sing and pray for their missing kin, salvation, peace, and forgiveness.

The following morning Dan entered the misty and damp street with a renewed vigour in his step and an upright proudness in his gait.

A smile stretched his mouth as earlier, waiting for him on the doorstep of the church, were additional supplies including dried fruits and meats, berries, and materials with which to make a hammock.

For the first time since his arrival in South Cave, he was greeted with a couple of nods and a solitary smile instead of the usual disregard and scornful glares as he walked the slope towards the graveyard.

He paused awhile at the ruined picket fence. The early morning sun had not lifted the grey mist from the realm of the dead, and all was eerily silent. The long grass swayed resplendent in the chilling breeze; on each blade, a shining globule of damp cast a red sparkle from dawn's fireball which slowly enlarged on the horizon.

In his fever one week ago, he hadn't noticed the decay of the boneyard nor the screeching of the solitary rusted gate hinge, which caused the morning birds to rise and flee from the unkempt wild grass.

Before entering, he paused and for a moment he studied, looking left, right, and ahead at the array of wooden markers, plaques, and headstone memorials that identified the killed in action, the diseased, the exhausted, the premature, the infected, and the accidental.

Joseph Hyde died 1837, J. P. Pender died 1860, Susanna McSweeney died 1842, Edwin Connell died 1851.

The laments continued and Dan dropped his head, closed his eyes, and quietly and flawlessly recited the words from Charles Garthwords: *'Heavenly Father, I call upon ye.'*

After half an hour of prayers silently recited at the grave of the young drummer boy, Dan arose, wiped clean his knees, and clutching his Bible tight within his grip, once more strode down Main Street with his neck stretched defiantly high and his eyes ardently fixed on the church ahead.

"You looking to occupy one of those?"

Recognising the voice, Dan ignored the skit from the shadow.

"Picking your patch, preach?" Dandridge continued, but as Dan inhaled the mid-morning breeze, he refused any temptation to respond.

Returning to the sanctuary, Dan occupied himself by making a broom, and as midday met the afternoon he busied himself by sweeping clear the months of decay that layered thick in the corners of the vestry.

He opened the main doors to allow the cloud of dirt to swirl out into the bright openness and, after clearing his lungs from the choke with the warm fresh waft, he briskly swept the pile of neglect out from the doors and down the steps.

Patting the dust free from his clothing, Dan's attention was drawn to an excitable gathering at the far end of the street near the Wild Hawk. He could see a couple of young men hollering and whooping just as he had witnessed a few days earlier with the hapless drummer boy.

He frowned with concern, and he sensed evil.

He watched the boardwalks filling quickly with spectators, and citizens roused by the noise hurried out onto the street with wide-eyed speculation.

He saw Jemima running in his direction and to her rear Issy followed, their faces flushed and eyes gaping.

Dan immediately recognised the look of alarm and fear.

They were shouting hysterically, but Dan could not interpret their distress until they collided with him.

With frenzied tears of anguish together they screamed words of uncontrolled rapidity which described that a couple of the town's unruly boys had seen half a dozen blue bellies resting by the stream near Bluebell Woods.

The frenzied boys, incited by Dandridge, Bill Todd, and Spivey, were urging South Cave's remaining men to gather their weapons and launch a surprise attack whilst the soldiers were at rest and still weary.

At first, Dan refused to get involved, but when he heard the distraught Jemima declare that Ray had taken the rabbit gun to join the murder squad, he gripped his Bible tight and set forth towards the upheaval. Watching the crowd's fervency, he sensed and feared the justice-seeking gathering was beyond any rationality and deep within he lacked any real conviction for being able to change the horde's minds, but obliging the two begging women who had previously helped him, he approached the armed mob of teenagers with a purposeful stride and a stiff regality.

Armed with pitchforks, knives, and a collection of decrepit-looking rifles, the young men were rallying loudly to a call of arms, and bolstered by the vocal and arm-waving Spivey, the boys were being worked up into an insane and senseless frenzy.

"Give 'em hell!" shouted Dandridge, his arm raised rousingly above his head as he charged down the street to join the group.

"Send them back to Washington or to hell. God cares for neither," he shouted without restraint.

"Put your guns away." Dan reached the crowd unnoticed and at first his call was not heard above the din. "Put away your guns!" he bellowed loudly, ducking under waving arms to enter the circle of bodies and approach the gun-wielding boys. "For all who draw their guns will die by the gun." He hailed, holding high his Bible for all to see. "Calm your fervour."

He spun on his heels to address all who surrounded him to watch with dismay.

"What the hell business is it of yours?" Spivey jumped down from the boardwalk and pulled back on stationary shoulders to clear his way.

"You cannot let your boys wander into mindless slaughter." Dan ignored Spivey and appealed to the elders whose boys faced peril.

The din began to quieten and the boys' commotion began to tame as Dan continued without pause. "Lay down your arms and return to your homes."

He turned towards the small gathering of armed boys. "Do not take revenge, for it is written." Looking confused, they began to lower their weapons as he quoted from the Bible. "The Lord said it is mine to avenge, and I will repay."

Dismayed frowns wandered and slackened jaws fell silent as Dan recited vociferously.

"Damn fine words for a preach who's from the other side," Spivey challenged loudly as he parted through the centre of the group to step in front of Dan. "And far away from his own land."

"My home is in the land of our God, as are all our homes." Dan's eyes met Spivey's and, standing face to face, their foreheads nearly collided.

"You can't allow this to happen," Dan warned. "Your boys will be slaughtered."

"Just trying to save more blue bellies from entering the gates of Hell." Spivey's eyes bulged with rage and hate.

"Your boys will be facing fighting men." Dan turned and opened his palm to plead again to the town's elders. "Seasoned fighters and natural killers." He spun and looked over Spivey's shoulder to shout at the onlookers beyond the back of the bully. "This will not be like going hunting."

"Ray! You listen to him." Jemima stepped out from the listeners to be near her son. "He speaks the truth." She reached out her hand in his direction and stretched her fingers, urging him to step towards her and away from his bewildered friends.

"No, Ma. I'm doing this for Pa." Ray stepped back and stood shoulder to shoulder with the rest of the boys.

Spivey nodded and grinned, then stood next to the boys with his fists superciliously resting on his hips.

"Ray, these targets will fire back." Dan pleaded directly to Ray.

"I beg you, Ray. Please." Jemima cried, and she placed her hand over her mouth to prevent herself from screaming.

Issy wrapped her arm around her ma's shoulder and threw her high tones in the boy's direction. "You don't know what you're doing. This is not your fight."

Dandridge sensed hesitation, and raising his fist again, he called out a rally for support. "Come on, boys. Let us send 'em off running with their tails between their legs!"

His bait worked, and euphoria again erupted from within the band of volunteers.

"Let's get to 'em!"

"Let's go get a Yank!"

"Send 'em for a swim in the Cumberland!"

They called out in unison to cheers and other boyish threats.

Spivey's satisfied grin opened his mouth so wide his crooked yellow teeth were displayed to Dan. "You better start praying for your Yankee friends, preach." He spat at Dan's feet.

"And maybe you might want to think about digging a few more holes over in Bluebell Woods for your friends." Dandridge winked as he wrapped a supportive arm around Ray's shoulder.

"Are you coming, Mr Dandridge?" one of the eager youngsters asked.

"Afraid not, my son." Dandridge shook his head to feign disappointment. "My eyes aren't too good for distance and anyways some of us need to stay put should a few of those Yanks come visiting us from down the Eastern trail."

"Are they that bad that you can't see death forthcoming?" Dan shouted over Spivey's shoulder to Dandridge.

"Keep out of our affairs, preach, before we turn our weapons on you." Dandridge's hand shaped into a pistol and pointed his fingers in Dan's direction.

"I am unarmed and I speak only the truth." Dan stepped past Spivey and opened out his arms wide in front of Dandridge; his body formed a cross.

"Well, your accuracies don't sit too well on this bank of the river," replied Dandridge.

Ballooning out his chest, Spivey again positioned himself between Dan and the boys. "Go and git out of our business before we start the killing right here."

Dan ignored the bully and refused to take a step back. "Ray, you must not go!" he shouted above the increasing din. "No one must go to Bluebell Woods." He turned again to the scowlers. "You must not allow this to happen." Then he focused again on Ray. "Some of you will not return." He shook his head.

Dandridge noticed hesitation again return to Ray's eyes. "You should be proud of your boys." His outstretched arm and the flat of his hand prevented Ray from stepping away from the gang and returning to Jemima. "And not be all watery-eyed like he's some little buck," he bellowed to the uncertain crowd.

"Stop him. Please stop him." Jemima screamed at the preacher.

"Ray! Listen to your ma." Dan's intended step forward was blocked by Spivey.

"I'm doing this for Pa." Ray's eyes brimmed with water and, embarrassed by the unwanted attention, he turned his face away from his mother's desperate imploring eyes. "I'm gonna make you proud, Ma. Just wait and see." He stepped backwards to find protection behind his friends.

"Ray, please!" Dan began, but the click of the cocked hammer distracted him.

"Off the street, preach, before you're lying face down in it."
Spivey held his pistol level to Dan's head.

Dan remained unmoved, his eyes searching beyond Spivey for the boy. "Ray, come out here."

The press of the steel increased to arch Dan's head back.

"Won't be asking so kindly next time, preach," Spivey warned. "Your words are done here. Nobody's listening to your advice, so now move away and get back in your cattle shed."

"Ray!"San shook his head, "I'm begging you. Please go home."

Spivey forced the barrel harder against Dan's forehead forcing him to move his feet backwards.

"Thats it preach, keep walking before my fingers slips and this trgger accidentally sends you into the clouds to parley with those blue bellies in the woods." Spivey grinned.

"Ray, you can't go. Listen to me." Dan's eyes still looked over Spivey's shoulder and he ignored the threat of death. "You are not a killer, Ray. You haven't been trained to kill."

The fervour began to wane and Dandridge sensed the hesitation returning in the boys as he watched the twitching of nervous fingers and the flicker of uneasy glances.

He narrowed his eyes and signalled a nod to Spivey. "No amount of training prepares you for the taking of lives, but come on, boys!" He raised his fist in the air. "Glory and everlasting honour await those who send Billy Yank running."

Spivey rapidly pulled back the pistol and swung it forward to sink deep into Dan's midriff.

Instantly Dan buckled and released a gasp. With his breath failing him he staggered backwards and his blurry vision prevented him from seeing Dandridge lunge forward to deliver a perfectly timed blow to his jaw.

Spinning sidewards, Dan did not see Spivey swing the pistol high, nor did he hear the crack of iron against his skull, nor did he feel the pain as light spiralled into darkness and he lost all his senses but hate.

In his failing consciousness, he could hear the rise of excited cheers and the call to arms of invigorated voices. He squinted hard and blinked repeatedly at the soil before him and, panting rapidly, he filled his lungs with reviving breaths to ensure the paralysis did not linger long.

Though all coordination was gone from his movements, he was able to clear his mind and hold off the head-spiralling pain just enough for him to haul himself up to one knee.

"Beware, my brethren, you are heading into the gates of hell," he whispered, watching distorted images of people loitering uneasily. Not too eager to slowly drift back to their occupations, listening to their muffled whispers of concern, he copied their stares along the trail which led the way to their boys on the distant hill near the cemetery.

Pain dictated that again he had to return his stare down to the soil in front of him and again he squinted several times to keep his vision clear.

He drew in more painkilling breaths and wiped the trickle of blood from the back of his head. Then, once the ground had stopped spinning, he forced every muscle in his body to haul him upright. Holding his gaze to the north and squinting towards the slope in the distance, he could still see the shadowy band of brothers, friends, and schoolboys reaching the summit of the track which led the way out of South Cave and toward the woodlands near the Cumberland.

Minds filled with glory, the boys strutted at speed with their heads held high and a spring in their heels, their conversation jolly and verbose with excited gestures and ignorant boasts.

Trickling blood began to warm the back of his neck as he watched the band of the doomed disappear over the hill. His fingers feathered the rising lump on the back of his head, but he ignored the pain and stretched out his hand to lift his Bible from the dirt. Then, lowering his eyes to the open pages of Psalms with forlorn disappointment, he sighed.

Large droplets of water began to dampen the pages and splatter into the soil. The rain broke his diversion, and he raised his face skywards to see bellowing stormy clouds darken the blue with thunderous rumbles forewarning of the impending deluge.

He closed his eyes and for a moment let God's wrath wet his face and he prayed as those around him fled for shelter, splattering mud as they passed him by.

"You should have stopped him!" a distraught Jemima shouted as she passed him by. "You should have stopped them all." She shook her head and sobbed into her hands. "You should have done more."

Dan's reply was lost in a deafening crack as the rain-filled clouds above collided. He turned and stood to call after her, but Jemima had been dragged away to cover by the linking arm of her daughter.

Chapter 9

The constant torrent of rain, flashes of lightning, and ground-shaking rumblings continued for most of the night, turning the dirt street into an unwalkable mire of mud.

Dan leaned upon the frame of the open doorway. From his position in the entrance of the restored church, he could just see through the vertical lashings, and twisting his neck left and right, he searched both directions of the street.

To his left, the din and raucousness of the Wild Hawk was muffled by the constant splattering of endless rain and the recurring rumbles from above. To his right, through the intermittent silver flashes of brilliance, he could see anxious ghostly faces peering wide-eyed through small windows, seeking and praying for the return of their loved ones. He groaned as from a distance he saw, through the relentless wide droplets, Jemima and Issy gazing north, their busy hands drying their tear-soaked cheeks with embroidered rags.

Eventually, the wind dragged the heavy clouds away eastwards, and replacing the howling rain and thunder emerged a band of morning orange that preceded the creeping sphere as it began to peek over the distant hills to displace the long shadows.

A thick mist formed from the departing murky damp as slowly the light crept along the streets and up the walls of buildings, but an eerie coldness lingered and a fretful silence lay over the stillness of the empty streets and boardwalks.

Dan had remained on the steps, his back slumped against the wood. He prayed for Jemima and Issy, the ignorant and the innocent, with his bible clutched tight to his chest, knowing the boys should have returned home well before the sun broke.

He sensed the inevitable doom, and his pulse galloped as he waited for the dreaded evil acknowledgment of death and butchery, and it was two hours later, on the distant slope, a silhouetted buckboard cart emerged against the orangey blue of the new day.

The tired, nauseated, but restless half a dozen parents who had gathered to comfort each other on the planks gawked in unity towards the slowly approaching cart as it swayed and struggled slowly forward through the deep mud.

More townsfolk began to appear on the boardwalks, and anxious neck stretches and long squints implored good news.

Dan watched Jemima and Issy run from their cabin to join the group across the mud, but he lost sight of them as they disappeared amongst a collection of frightened hugs and consoling embraces.

Dandridge appeared and casually sauntered to lean on his usual hitch rail and, further down the street, Spivey yawned and stretched out his tired limbs.

Dan considered joining the worried relatives, but he knew he would not be welcomed, so he just stretched out tall, kissed the leather on his bible, and watched the cart, begging for good news.

Suddenly, and in the same instant as he experienced a throat-drying fear, ear-piercing screams penetrated his ears to confirm the horror he dreaded.

The cart had drawn close to the edge of town and within the view of the gatherers. His stomach reeled, and a grimness rose within. He couldn't swallow, and his hands shook uncontrollably. He watched two women pass out, others fall to their knees screaming, and one solitary mother sped towards the cart with a horrifying lack of all gracefulness.

Contorted grimaces of revulsion whitened their anguished cheeks as, emerging into everyone's view, was the devil's death transporter.

Piled high with lifeless bodies of young fools, the grim reaper at the tiller pulled the horse to a halt at the edge of the boardwalk as the bereft woman fell to her knees, blocking its passage.

Within what seemed an endless moment, the rush of wailing and distraught loved ones surged forward to surround the cart and completely block any progress.

"They were God-damned bushwhacked." Dan heard the death carrier shout. "Yankees waiting for them in the thicket a few miles short of Bluebell."

Some threw themselves to their knees, pleading and spatting their wrath upon the Lord, whilst others stretched out their hands against the cold skin of the dead.

Gasps of disbelief, more piercing screams of agony, and relentless screams reached every street corner and stretched far and wide above the barren rain-soaked fields and distant peaks.

Dan walked with his head angled low past the inconsolable, who hugged with shrieks and tears, knowing they had all failed the ignorance of youth. For a moment he said nothing.

He simply looked at the lifeless pile of young men who had been prematurely hurled into eternity, then he closed his eyes to curse Satan.

Not positioned to serve any purpose, the dead boys had just been callously dumped on top of each other with their heads buried between the folds of their blood-stained clothes. Ashen faces with painful death grimaces stared blankly into the afterlife, and sagging loose was the visible flesh of protruding hands and leather-stripped bare feet. Dripping from the cart to speckle patterns in the puddles below was a cascade of red.

Sickened at the sight of the barbarism, Dan clasped his hands tight and closed his eyes to pray.

"Are they on their way here?" shouted a pale-faced old-timer.

"No." The cart man dabbed his damp forehead with a bloody rag. "Cowards must have skedaddled before there could be any consequences."

No one other than the immediate families of the dead had shown themselves, and no one from the town offered any help or consolation. Flint Spivey and Tyree Dandridge watched the distress from a distance whilst everyone else seemed to be suddenly busy with their occupations. No one moved to assist, and no one offered any comfort or sympathy.

"Will you set my boy?" a blood-veined, teary-eyed woman softly asked Dan from beneath the cover of her scarf, which hid most of her face.

He answered with a simple nod.

"Some are too afraid to ask." The one-legged veteran raised his head from his wet hands. "But we'd all be mighty grateful if you'd do the same for us."

"I'll prepare a service for tonight."

Jemima and Issy reached out towards the cart. A limp hand was dangling over the side of the wood barrier. Although the face of the body was obstructed, Jemima instinctively knew Ray's small palm.

"Where is your God now? Why didn't he help?" she wailed through bleary eyes to Dan.

"You could have done more." She lifted the white hand against her lips and kissed it whilst holding a forlorn glare to Dan.

"You should have stopped them." She screamed at Dan, then dropping her knees into the reddened mud, she threw her face skywards and bawled bitterly at the Lord, the Devil, Lincoln, Jefferson Davis, and the Reverend Dan Earl with equal abhorrence borne from her uncontrollable grief.

Dan knew she was right. God had abandoned them, and he should have tried harder to draw God's will. He closed his eyes again and bowed his head with a gentle shake. He was a war veteran who knew the boys' misadventure was doomed. He also knew comforting words from the Lord's book were not welcome right now. His remorse was plain to see and his guilt riled him, but neither knowing what to say to Jemima nor how to say it, he simply kept his head low and asked Issy gently,

"Will you please get me the names of all the boys?" He placed his hand gently on her shoulder. "There'll be a service tonight."

Helping Issy to haul her ma from the mud, Dan then climbed up beside the cart handler. "Let's take these boys home."

"I don't need your help, pastor." The grey-whiskered man declined as he tried to wipe the blood of the dead from his bib.

"Lead! Lead on." Dan raged with an uncompromising glare.

As the cart ploughed through the mud on Main Street, Dan was certain he saw something in the carpenter's expression. His eyes seemed to narrow and a slight crease in his cheeks betrayed his false sympathies as the wagon of the dead passed him by. Dan cussed to himself, 'avarice is the vice of all evil'.

He held a scowl to display his disapproval, but his attention was agitated by Dandridge, who hollered another warning as the cart drew alongside to his hitch rail.

"Don't you be clawing your rotten paws into our widows now, preach." Dan's eyes remained on the track ahead. "We've heard you've got a liking for vulnerable young widows."

He tried to ignore the snidely threats, and he allowed his eyelids to rest for a moment. It had been a long time since he thought of poor Nettie, and clamping his teeth to force restraint, he clenched his hands into tight balls until his knuckles whitened, but a chuckle from the man seated by his side rattled him from his brief reminisce.

'Go to hell!' he thought, keeping his lips tight.

One by one, Dan and the driver, who remained unfriendly and nameless, silently returned the dead to their homes.

From one solitary candle-lit small room, he moved on from cabin to cabin to haul and lay out on tables, boards, and planks the boys who had, a few hours earlier, been condemned to the eternal sleep. Prayers were said and coins placed over eyes to cover the glassy skyward glare, but no words were spoken by those who were suffering the great affliction.

Sensitive mumblings, cries, and shrieks of lamented wailing and mourning were heard from almost every cabin, but no one heard or listened to the words of prayer and oration which were earnestly repeated by the northern preacher who kneeled at the side of all the dead. Even Jemima and Issy did not raise their heads to acknowledge the preacher who stayed by their sides until near dark to pray for their strength and fortitude.

By darkness, Dan waited on the steps of the holy house with his bible clutched to his chest and his sermon set within his mind. He stood in silence, waiting apprehensively to receive the mourners who defied the will of Dandridge and Spivey to brave the walk across the mud.

As the minutes closed in on the call to worship, the opening of door hinges rasped and creaks of wooden planks sounded as, slowly appearing from the shadows, were the shrouded arched figures of the lost and grieving.

Dan straightened his back as the two dozen or so darkened figures began to near him.

His eyelids closed them out briefly, and he moaned to God. 'Why did it need such evil to open their eyes to you?'

Relentless sobs wailed continuously as pairs and small groups, all leaning on each other for support dejectedly, staggered towards the candles that brightened the entrance around the small temple of reckoning.

"You all turn yourselves around now and head back to your homes!" hollered out of the darkness across the street.

Startled and pausing with hesitation, the mourners turned their swollen eyes to see Dandridge and Bill Todd step down to the mud.

"No one's going anywhere tonight." Dandridge strode to the middle of the street, halting directly opposite the church.

"That's right." Todd supported ominously, balancing his rifle on his shoulder.

"We need to pray more than ever tonight." Jemima beseeched.

"Then pray at your bedside because no one's going into the traitor's lair." Spivey hollered from the street corner, his location confirmed by the glow of his cigar.

"God's heart welcomes you." Dan Earl defiantly declared from the doorway. "Please listen to your hearts and come."

He opened out his arms wide to invite the grief-stricken, then he angled his body to face Spivey. "Their words need to be heard by God."

"And so they shall, but from their bedsides and the side of the dead." Spivey flicked the stub into the mud and stepped on the hiss. "And not by the side of our enemy." He damned as he walked towards Dandridge and Todd.

"Blessed shall you be when you come into the house of the Lord, and blessed you shall be when you go out." Dan called out.

An explosion noise and the flash of powder jolted the small procession to a halt and, raising their ghostly faces to the brief flare, they hesitated to take another step.

"You welcomed in the devil and he delivered death to your door." Dandridge condemned, holding his pistol towards the stars.

"You should have heeded my warnings about this devil." Spivey curved his walk away from Dandridge and headed towards the bottom of the church steps. "Satan disguises himself in many forms."

He placed one foot on the lower step and angled his face at the candle-illuminated preacher.

"Even as an angel of the light." He then trod the second step to obstruct Dan from the mourners, then he twisted at the waist to wave his pistol above the heads of the afraid. "Now turn about and return to your boys, for no one is climbing these steps tonight."

"Drop your gun and get away from my church." Dan had withdrawn the pistol Jemima gave him from beneath his cassock, and he pressed the barrel against Spivey's spine.

Spivey grinned and, shaking his head knowing the pastor no longer had a gun, he laughed. "Think me a fool."

"Only a fool would ignore the wisdom of a gun." Dan silenced Spivey's laugh by clicking the hammer.

"You see this! A man of God who raises a gun." Spivey shouted to Dan's disciples.

"Ain't that just what my sister wrote us?" Todd swung the rifle from his shoulder and levelled it at Dan. "Beware the devil in sheep's clothing." He shouted loudly. "She warned us all."

He firmed his finger on the trigger, but he knew in the dark and with Spivey obstructing the target his aim was untrue. "Her letters were clear."

"You said yourself the gun is more powerful than the words of God." Dan pressed the barrel until Spivey arched his back and winced. "Now, drop your gun and get away from my church."

"I warned you he was a killer!" Todd squinted down the barrel.

"You going to take us all?" Dandridge shouted, also taking aim.

Buoyed by his friend's defiance, Spivey resisted Dan's force and he twisted his face to threaten. "I think you'll be singing with the dead tonight, preach." Within an instant, and to astonished gasps below, Dan swung his pistol hard against the back of Spivey's skull and, as the man sagged and his legs buckled, Dan kicked him with the flat of his foot to cast him face down in the mud.

Before Dandridge and Todd could react, Dan had jumped down from the steps, away from the hue of the candles, and rolled across the mud to rise with his back straight and his pistol inches from Dandridge's face.

"If it's God's will, then I reckon so." He replied unnervingly.

Todd's eyes flicked sideways, and he whispered to Dandridge. "I don't doubt that."

Keeping his eyes fixed and his aim true, Dan called out, "Jemima. You lead the way." He beckoned with his left arm. "The others will follow."

Noticing Jemima gently raise the hem of her skirt from the mud, Dandridge ordered, "Don't you move a step, Jemima. His kind has already taken your boy." All three men held their weapons firm. "Don't let them take your soul as well."

"You brought forth our boys' deaths." She snapped. "You roused them on with talk of glory and honour."

With his aim remaining determined, Dan's eyes flashed between Dandridge and Todd.

"What no. This imposter from the north showed the enemy the way to our door."

"Our enemy was in this town long before he arrived."

Lusting for Jemima and still harbouring ambitions to lure her into a relationship, Dandridge deliberated his next move. His thoughts were divided and strained as he speculated whether to rid the town of the holy nuisance who had resurrected Jemima's inner strength and given her renewed hope or to show the preacher mercy.

He knew Jemima's mindset was almost crushed and by removing her spiritual leader, he would destroy all of her last vestiges of strength and make her easy prey for his shameless desires.

Within a few days, she would finally be under his control for him to manipulate her thoughts however he wished.

He also contemplated that he would gain her respect and rise in her esteem if he offered amnesty and allowed the preacher to walk away unharmed.

Finally, he decided death could be delivered another day, without witnesses. Boldly, he lowered his pistol, but keeping his eyes locked on Dan, he reached out to press Todd's rifle down to the mud.

Todd snarled an objection and grunted something inaudible, but Dandridge signalled with a leer that his authority must be followed, then confidently he walked the few steps to stand in front of Jemima.

"Don't be fooled by Lucifer's words of seduction." He said, then testing her loyalty he glared into her eyes and, smiling, he placed his hand on her shoulder. "Ignore this devil's urge and return to your home."

"I no longer have a home. Just an empty cabin." She quivered.

Dan raised his eyebrows and slanted his head towards the church door.

Jemima recognised his will, and she forced away the detaining hand to tread towards the entrance steps.

Issy grasped her hand to follow on behind, but the rest of the mourners were now reluctant to proceed.

Seeing the indecision within the mourners, Dan lowered his gun. He knew they were already afraid and the display of weapons had increased their anxieties.

"Remember our Lord also lost his only son. Trust in him and he will act." Dan shouted.

"Never can reconcilement grow where the wounds of deadly hate have pierced so deep." Dandridge bellowed as he turned to face the worshippers.

Dropping their heads to their feet to avoid the eyes of the preacher, most of the hurt and grieving halted their short journey.

Dandridge noticed their uncertainty and, bolstered by their frailty, he roared, "Do not listen to the words of the traitor! Return to your homes and pray by the side of your sons."

Only the two elderly widows and the cripple followed Jemima's and Issy's lead. The rest delayed and, buoyed by their reluctance, Dandridge would not relent.

"Be careful who you trust. The devil was once an angel."

"Our struggle is not against the devil." Dan appealed. "It is against the flesh and blood of men like you." He raised a finger at Dandridge. "His servants."

A crooked woman with a hunched back hissed at the cripple near Jemima and, after a cuss in return, he begrudgingly turned to splash his crutch into the mud and rejoin the pack. They turned in unison, slowly beginning to trudge silently back to their cold, unwelcoming miserable homes.

"You'll regret the day you raised a gun to Tyree Dandridge." The bully ensured the preacher understood the matter was not yet over.

"I have many regrets. But with God's grace, I fear nothing." Dan snarled and boldly swept his gun to his rear. Then tucking it into his belt, he turned his back to the two menaces to escort the women towards the church.

"God did not spare angels when they sinned." Dandridge ominously forewarned. "He will not spare you and when your judgment is pronounced, you will join them in the eternal darkness of the underworld."

Not knowing whether he would receive a bullet in the back or not, Dan inhaled a muscle-bracing breath, then without further hesitation, he ignored the threat and followed the four women up the steps. From the height of the last step, he glanced over his shoulder to glimpse Todd hauling a groggy and disorientated Spivey out of the mud.

Closing the door behind him, he watched the mourners produce and light more candles, which they carefully sealed with hot wax on the makeshift altar. Whilst they sobbed and prayed, Dan raised himself on the pulpit to begin his sermon.

With his eyes closed, he recited calmly and flawlessly. "I am the light of the world. Whoever follows me will not walk in the shadow of darkness, for they will have the light of life, and those who inflict evil will go forth into eternal punishment whilst the righteous will grace eternal life."

For forty minutes Dan tried to search for the right words for this sad and grievous time.

He hailed God's words of hope to aid and comfort the sufferers before him and he delivered prayers for those who were too afraid to sit by the side of their anguished neighbours on the row of crates beneath him.

"Mourn not the passing of a life, but celebrate." His tone was faint and his words were delivered with tenderness and not in his usual vigorous rhyme.

"Celebrate the times when you laughed, played, and loved together. Celebrate when you helped each other and the times when you needed to reach out and touch each other's soul." He paused to allow the sobs to soften a little. "Death is only the end of a chapter and as the soul leaves the body and makes its return to God's kingdom, its spirit will watch over you and live with you forever in your heart. It will bring recollections and times of sadness as you all adapt to the passing of one so close and one so loved."

He then had to raise his voice as the wailing of grief increased. "Yet this is part of your life. You must go on and walk in the land of the living, and we must continue every day until God's beckoning calls us forth.

And whilst in these moments of dark anguish, when it feels as if there is only silent pain and endless nights of suffering, memories of the good times will see us through until the new dawn's rising wakens our souls with a fresh desire and a promise of newfound conviction."

Suddenly, Dan fell silent, and he paused. His chosen words were obliterated by confusion and his vision hazed. He grabbed hold of the wooden frame to rebalance himself and he gasped in air repeatedly to compose himself as the worshippers in front of him faded into darkness.

He shook his head and squinted, then finally the colour of his sight began to return, but before him was not the dimness of the church or the orange hue sprayed out from candles.

His vision was bright with different shades of green and brown.

Again he shook his head, but he could not repel from his sight the dense woods and tall trees which surrounded his home in North Cave, nor could he repel the emergence of the dream which dictated his passage to the South Cave.

Penetrating deep into his subconscious was the sight of the death cart transporting the loose hanging limbs of the ashen-faced dead boys. He sighed and arched over to his side as his stomach tightened beyond his control and vomit began to rise from within.

The glassy eyes of the young dead fixed upon him and the piercing screams of bereaved stabbed bolts of pain in his temples.

"Are you alright?" asked Issy, but his blank face did not respond.

His chest rose and sank rapidly as uncontrolled repeated pants and shallow bursts of breath paralysed him. He felt the flat of a consoling palm rest on his back between his shoulders and another hand touched his chest.

His eyes remained distracted, his pupils large and black. He did not respond to her comfort.

"Pastor, are you in pain?" Jemima now stood by his side.

A drum rolled past his feet and he screamed. "I've failed them. I've failed God."

"Do you need the doctor?" This time he slanted his grimaced face towards Issy and he staggered upright. She firmed her hold and Jemima grabbed his elbow and forearm.

His breathing slowed and the spiralling vision of the dead began to fade. He frowned at Issy as if he did not recognise her, and his scowl scared her.

"Do you need the doctor?" she repeated with a noticeable tremble.

"No." He finally stammered. "I'm sorry. Please forgive me." He shook his head. "Please return to your seat. I'll be alright in a moment."

Jemima placed in front of him a jug of water and he sipped, then looking up he drew in long calming vapours of her scent and sighed. Why did he not remember, how could he forget, why did he not realise that he had been sent by God to prevent the slaughter of the South Cave boys and the hanging of the drummer boy and not simply to listen to the prayers of the frail and needy? He had failed God, the dead, and the grief-stricken.

He wandered in a solitary realm of silence, wondering what he should do now, until the lamenting sobs of the elderly widows to his front jolted him. He forced a thankful smile to Jemima and Issy and gestured for them to be seated so that he could return to the service.

The vision was now clear to him, but being obsessed with repairing the church and acting as a reformer, he knew he had neglected his duties. He wondered what he should do now. His urging was to walk away from the church and leave South Cave, but as his vision cleared and he saw the agonised faces before him, he knew he could not abandon them and withdraw the courage they needed and sought from God.

Taking another sip of water whilst the women tentatively took up their positions on the crates, Dan composed himself and reopened his bible, then inducing a cough to clear his throat, he began. "Together, we will wipe the tears from your eyes." At first, his voice was weak, but after another sigh and a large lung fill of air, he continued on with a disguised spirit. "There will be no more mourning, crying, or pain, for God is by your side and he hears your prayers. He will give you courage and he will heal your fears, and today's suffering will reunite and bring us together for eternal life in our Father's kingdom."

He knew all the ears were numb to his final words of compassion and no thoughts were set for entering heaven, but he had done his duty and abided by God's will for tonight.

His last words as the small congregation departed were that he would be present at the cemetery tomorrow to deliver their sons and brothers into the house of eternal peace. His offer received four subdued nods of appreciation and tearful flutters of reluctant acceptance, but as he walked down the centre of the church and opened the door in his usual polite way, tonight there were no handshakes, no fond regards, no praise and no gratitude, just slanted deliberate glances and expressions of acceptance and toleration.

He stood on the steps above the street, watching the bereaved and the widows huddle together as they silently stepped from the side planks and down onto the mud to make their return to their inhospitable small homes.

He was distressed by the slaughter and sorrowful he did not prevent it, but he was also saddened that Jemima and Issy had not spoken to him or bid him good night upon their departure.

He sucked in the chilly night breeze and sighed, knowing he had failed them all, and just as his mind sank into deep contemplation for tomorrow's internments, a cold blast of night breeze swung the doors, causing them to loudly slam shut. Jolted from his meditations, Dan turned to retire and prepare for the early morning, but just as he flicked one more glance over his shoulder, a jaundiced splash of light briefly caught his eye.

He held his attention at the Wild Hawk in the distance just enough to see the shape of a man leaning on the hitch rail, but just as quickly as the shadow revealed itself, it vanished again into the blackness as the swinging door of the saloon returned the street to darkness.

He was about to dismiss the gazer and return to the church when the sound of distant hooves troubled him.

He held his grip on the door, but he did not pull it open to enter the church.

The rapidity of mud splattering and stomping hooves riveted him to the deck, and he squinted into the dark to determine the approaching rider.

Head held low and urging the beast on at a gallop, at first Dan thought the man may be rushing to deliver news, but he became alarmed when the rushing horseman bounded past the Wild Hawk and continued perilously down the almost empty street.

He switched his eyes to the trudging broken-hearted shadows who stood in the rider's line of direction, heads hung low and minds lost amidst the hollowness of what greeted their return within their homes. They did not at first hear the danger approaching. Dan yelled and, turning their heads with identicalness, fear emblazoned itself upon their faces and they froze to an immovable hardness, realising the huge creature just a few yards away was striding directly towards them.

With only time to clamp shut their eyes, the thunder of hooves and the breath from wide savage nostrils was upon them as the beast ploughed straight into them, hurling bodies, snapping bones, and spinning legs and arms high into the air.

Dan could not prevent his hand from clamping tight over his eyes, nor could he stop his teeth from grinding hard and his legs buckling beneath him as the sickening crunch of shattering bone befell upon his ears.

Echoing screams displaced the unabated thud of hooves as, regaining its gait, the speeding horse continued ahead until it disappeared into the pitch of the distance.

Dan leaped from the steps, his feet clearing the planks to stumble in the mud. Unaware he had dropped his bible, he sprung up from his knees and scrambled to the scattered wrecked bodies. He scanned quickly across all four women, then his eyes stopped on the two women who were vaulted and spun violently high. Instantly he knew death claimed another soul as, reaching and turning over the body of one of the bonneted women, her head dangled loose and her body sagged lifeless in his hands. He lowered the woman gently and crawled on his knees across to the other motionless body.

Carefully again, he turned the body over, then closing his eyes he raged with uncontrolled anger at God for the first time in many years as he realised beneath the muddy mask was the spiritless face of Issy.

He cradled her body and flung his head back to scream skywards, fearing she had expired, but as water filled his eyes, a warm gust from her lungs breezed on his exposed, stretched neck. Instantly, he dropped his head lower to her face.

"She's alive! She's alive!" he shouted, but then doubt instantly vexed him as he thought maybe it was just her last breath being expelled as he disturbed her body.

He gently raised her shoulders and cupped her head with his shaky hand, then he lowered his face again to meet her mouth.

He held both the grip and his breath until finally his face warmed with another faint breath.

He looked around for help and pleaded wildly into the darkness for help.

Stunned, and with her equilibrium scrambled beyond immediate recovery, Jemima tried to rise from the mire, but with her faculties disobeying her, she succumbed to collapsing and dropped her face into her cupped hands.

Gradually Dan's call penetrated the monotonous hum within her ear and she began to slowly stagger to her knees.

Unable to rise from her crawling position, she squinted across at her motionless daughter and the man with the devil's anger in his eyes. Her dazed gaze flickered between the limp girl and the unrecognisable ghostly face with the dense black piercing eyes.

She did not recognise this stranger who shouted words in her direction and she could not understand what he was repeating, but hesitantly she dragged herself closer.

Still stunned and confused, her mind was unable to comprehend why, in the middle of this muddy carnage, her daughter was cradled in the arms of a man whose soul had transitioned into a demon.

"She's alive! She's alive! Jemima! She's alive. Help somebody! Please help." Slowly the buzzing hum subdued and the plea of the devil began to reverberate within her mud-filled ears.

The crazed man waved one arm frantically, beckoning her towards him as he yelled relentlessly. Oblivious to her own pain, but fearing her daughter was near to death, Jemima clenched her teeth and hesitantly took to her knees and dragged herself towards the extended hands of the angry man to accept the limp body.

As he straightened and twisted to quickly scan across the wooden frontages and boardwalks, his stare briefly fell upon her wet eyes. A chill flashed down her spine as in the blackness of his pupils she saw the flames of hellfire and a soul filled with retribution.

The old cripple appeared and he cussed as his deficient eyes scrutinised the butchery.

"Accident?" he questioned.

Dan's fierce glare was absolute and the old-timer deliberated, his fingers stroking his white beard until his vision adjusted to the darkness and the full horror appeared in front of him.

Expanding his lungs to bellow out repeated calls for help, he banged his crutch against the door behind him, then he hobbled down to the mud and knelt by the side of his dead neighbour.

Dan yelled as cautious onlookers gathered, but hesitated to help. There was a silent reluctance and an obvious unwillingness to help.

Incensed by the rebuttal, Dan bounded up from the mud and pounced on the side planks.

"God's judgement will be upon you all!" Enraged by their passive acceptance of the bullies' domination, he spat in the faces of the cowards who dithered nervously.

"Do not betray your Lord."

Dumbfounded by their unwillingness to help, he found it necessary to place his hands on the shoulders of the onlookers to shake them. He rushed from one pallid face to another, urging them to help the injured.

"The eyes of the Lord are on you!" He opened out his hands to the darkness above as his rage strengthened.

"Do not withhold when it is in your power to act." Shuddering with fear from the maniac's display, slowly steps were taken towards the street.

"He who watches all will not forget."

Dan continued relentlessly urging for help until his intimidation overwhelmed the old-timer's fear of retaliation from Spivey and Dandridge, and so with slow, uncertain steps eventually they descended onto the street to wrap their arms gently around the injured.

From the boards on high, Dan looked down and watched as the elderly raised the bruised and covered the dead with an accompaniment of damning forewarnings and murmurings reiterating their earlier prophecy.

Issy was prised from the arms of Jemima and carried from view whilst the two who were just able to walk were assisted back to the sanctuary and the safety within their cabins.

Near silence was soon restored upon the place of murder. Only muffled disorder leaked through the walls of the Wild Hawk in the distance to disturb the howling swirl of the cool evening gusts and the faraway calls of the lonely night creatures.

Dan trudged the thick mud back to the church alone with his ears echoing the thunderous pounding of the charging beast and the piercing screams of the doomed women. He closed his eyes, lowered his head, and for a moment he stopped to shake away the horror, but as he reopened his eyes his angered vision locked onto the flickering white pages of his bible.

Instant dread soared through his fibre, knowing Nettie's hair must be gone and now forever lost. He arched his back and scoured the darkness without success, then with care he lifted the leather binding from the mire.

An uncontrolled roar burst out from his lungs when, flicking his muddy fingers through the pages, his fear was confirmed and the memento was gone forever. He clamped the book tight and scraped off the mud from his sole before treading the steps to enter the stillness of the church and slumping down to rest his back against a crate.

Anger again replaced God's influence and wisdom within. He clasped his hands together and bowed his head to dispel all ungodly insertions and thoughts of hate and revenge, but he found no solace, only fury. Coldness had displaced all his profundity and the warmth of his temperament. His mind had become possessed by the alchemy from the brutal attack on the innocent worshippers.

"In the sorrow of death is the proof of love." He began to pray, but his thoughts began to wander. "God gives me the right to protect my worshippers."

The prayer subsided into faithlessness, and his mind filled with the image and memories of the charging horse. Over and over the thud of the hooves, the sound of the galloping pants, and the snap of bones occupied his mind.

The vision repeated within the dark room and it recapitulated the horse galloping by the Wild Hawk at the far end of the street and thundering past his numbed and helpless body outside the church to obliterate the innocent figures whose shock and fear had held them mute and static.

Again the darkened horse came into his view at the saloon, but this time Dan's recollections and concentration switched to the shadowy figure leaning on the hitch rail next to the saloon door as a flicker of yellow lamplight exposed Dandridge's face. As the rider sped by him, Dan studied the memory over again and again. The rapid splash of light from the swinging of the saloon door was brief, but it was enough to reveal Dandridge's face.

Dan held his head in his hand as he recalled the nightmare and shuddered in almost disbelief when this time he saw Dandridge mantle an ear-to-ear sinister grin. On the fifth and sixth observation, he saw Dandridge raise his head and nod an acknowledgment at the passing horseman.

With his body shaking in silent emotion as he grieved, Dan shook his head and the pit of his stomach turned. The revelation confirmed Dandridge knew the killer.

Once more he called upon his recollections to replay the intentions of the charging horseman. The black horse roared past him and scattered bodies with a destructive impact over and over and time and time again until, in the blink of an eye, emerged a glimpse of a Kepi. He wondered if he was hallucinating and he doubted the imagery as he sought out the killer.

He considered his recollections as being judicious towards Spivey and Dandridge and he needed to blame someone, so he thought perhaps his subconscious bias had distorted his recollections. Suddenly a gust of wind levered then slammed the door, shaking the rickety slats and forcing Dan's painful memories back into his subconscious.

The resulting blast of cold air jolted Dan to arise and stretch out from his intense brooding to close the door. However, reaching the creaking door, something compelled him to place an eye close to the narrow open gap and peer in the direction of the Wild Hawk.

A shudder spasmed down his spine and his eyes widened with alarm.

He held the flat of his palm against the wood to prevent the door from hindering his view of the solitary horse which had been secured outside the Wild Hawk.

Without hesitation, Dan abandoned the church and sped down the centre of the street, the high moon reflecting his bounding shadow in the shiny mud.

The horse reared a little and neighed, but with a calming stroke of its mane and some hushed comforting words its agitation soon quelled and Dan was able to examine it with the use of his hands. The horse's neck and flank were wet with sweat and its chest was dripping with a thicker and darker liquid.

Dan rubbed his fingers through the dark wetness and held them to the sky where a brief glint of moonlight confirmed blood. He snarled words of hate and walked towards the saloon door where he could hear garrulous chatter from beyond the wood. He wrapped his fingers around the door handle and drew breath, but unexpectedly the words of his mentor resonated in his thoughts and he paused. 'Do not overcome evil with evil.' Then he felt God whisper the commandments into his ear. 'You shall not murder.' He lowered his head and released his hand from the door handle. 'Resist the devil.'

"God of vengeance, I call upon thee to shine forth." He whispered and for a moment he closed his eyes and wiped his brow as he deliberated. "God will come." Again he murmured, then as the mirth from the saloon again replaced the summons of God, he took a dejected step back.

Finally, the satanic desire for retribution that burned within faded, and shaking his head he turned his back to the saloon. "I must not put the Lord, my God, to the test."

Striding with purpose, Dan did not return immediately to the church. He stopped at the undertaker's and kicked in the door, then with a shovel in his hand he marched toward the cemetery where, under the silver canopy of the stars, he wildly hollowed out thirteen graves.

Chapter 10

Dan sat alone in the darkness, stroking his thumb across his inflamed blisters. By dawn, he had completed the new graves, and by noon he had laid to rest ten young boys and the murdered worshipper.

By dark, he cleaned up Jemima's old gun with bacon fat and he had tried to rest, but sleep avoided him as he struggled to repress his increasing frustration and a sense of inadequacy. His path ahead was no longer clear. His visions had returned and his failures to prevent the slaughters haunted him.

"They won't stop until you're either gone or dead." He did not hear Jemima's footsteps in the open doorway; his preoccupation had consumed his senses.

"What are you doing here?" He swivelled his neck.

"You haven't eaten." Jemima held out the familiar linen-covered basket.

He smiled and began to rise from his slouch. "Shouldn't you be with Issy?"

"I'm not staying." She replied quickly.

"How is she?" Through the dimness, he saw the puffiness in her eyes.

"Bruised and very sore, but the Doc says she's going to be ok with plenty of bed rest." She bent her knees to place the basket on the crate in front of him.

"I wanted to visit, but..."

"I know." She cut him off, knowing the chat would have only brought more trouble upon them both.

"I'm sorry. This is all my fault." With the apology, he took a step towards her.

"I shouldn't have come here and tried to bestow my beliefs on this town."

"I know you're hurting, but don't blame yourself for this. This isn't your doing." Her tone was soft, but troubled. "This town was long beyond any salvation before you came." She did not draw back from his approach. "You've done what you can for this town. It's beyond any redemption."

Dan was now just a few inches away from her.

"It was Spivey." He announced plainly.

"I saw his face." She confirmed. "Just before the horse hit Issy." She paused before exhaling. "I saw him grinning at us with death in his eyes."

Dan was right. The flashback was true.

Bile rose from within and he turned quickly to splatter retch over his boots, knowing Spivey and Dandridge had plotted to deliberately kill their innocent neighbours as revenge for their disobedience.

Jemima rested her fingers on his back as he arched.

"Why?" Dan shook his head and frowned as he returned upright.

"They slay their own to make people fear them for no more than ego, greed, and authority."

"It is a callous heart that takes and destroys the life of his kinfolk."

"These men do not possess a heart."

Dan pulled free a canteen from the basket and pulled off the top to swill his mouth and cool his throat.

"Dandy's a coward." He swallowed.

"But he is ruthless." Jemima warned. "Whilst all our men are away readily accepting to end their days and sacrifice their all in the hope of better days for their loved ones back home, he and Spivey stayed behind to bully and profiteer under the banner of the Militia. Now they slay for pure evil and greed, not for liberty."

Jemima rested on the crate, and Dan sat beside her.

"I'm guessing Spivey blames everyone for the loss of his son."

"Even God himself." She confirmed.

"He has no humanity. Only hate, and instead of any empathy for the suffering folk around here, he has only anger. The only happiness he seems to find is from being spiteful to those who are nearest of kin."

"Has he always been this way?" Dan still wondered if he could bring Spivey salvation. "Was he this way before he lost the boy?"

"He has never been what you'd call a good man in this town." She recalled. "He's a murdering bully who sought to profiteer from the weak. Now the guilt haunts him."

"Guilt?" Dan was confused.

"He should have protected his son, like all of us should. They were too young to give up their lives for this war. Yet whilst, with every breath, we fight against bitterness to find forgiveness for our enemies, he chooses the tune of hatred and he dances with the devil to bring his damnation upon the whole town."

"Hatred will not ease grief and without grief, his abomination will not wilt." Dan reasoned, but he knew inside Spivey's soul was destined for Hades.

"There are no lions here to tame him." She bemoaned the loss of all the fighting men. "Only scheming coyotes."

"I fear any lingering shadow of faith he may have harboured has departed for good." Dan admitted.

Suddenly gunfire sounded outside and the thud of lead ripped near to the door.

"Folks are saying you dug two extra graves, preacher!" bellowed from the darkness behind the church doors.

Dan and Jemima instantly ducked low, but remaining silent their eyes widened and locked onto each other for longer than they normally would.

"Is it true?" Spivey shouted. "Two holes!"

The pistol shot roared, splitting another wood panel.

"Is it right, preach? What I've been hearing." Spivey continued his rant. "Who they for? You got something you want to say to me or maybe you're figuring it's time you did a little more than talking."

Another shot was discharged.

"You got a message from God?" Spivey sniggered loudly.

Dan drew in a deep breath and shuffled uneasily on the crate.

"Get out here and face me, preacher. You and your God against me. Two versus one." A fourth shot roared. "All equal and fair."

Another blast soon followed. "Don't you think?"

"He won't come in here." Jemima revealed. "He won't do the devil's work in the house of worship." She placed her hand firmly on top of his to stop his fingers tapping on the crate. "You're safe here." Her eyes contained reassurance.

"Let us equal the odds and make it fair. Two versus two." Bill Todd stepped down from the boardwalk balancing a rifle nonchalantly on his shoulder. "You and the mighty against us humble southern patriots."

Dan slid out his hand from under her palm and, placing his hands on her shoulders, he asked her to stay seated, then with silent footsteps, he neared the door.

A loud creak in the door alerted Spivey, and he knew the preacher was peering at him through the small breach.

"Son of a bitch." He sneered wildly.

Dan watched the gunman drag in tobacco from his cigar, then place the lit smoke behind his ear to reload his pistol. Dan flicked a glance towards Todd, then alarmingly he found his attention diverted to two bottles, which were fixed in the mud next to the troublemaker's feet.

"Please come away." Jemima stood alongside the man in black, and she too glimpsed briefly through the narrow gap.

"Come away from the door. It's safer back here." She whispered.

"This must end." Dan replied.

"They're drunk." She sensed the fever in Dan's spirit. "They'll tire and they will go home soon." She tried to protect him by lying.

"Come out, preach!" Spivey levelled the reloaded weapon and fired at the gap. "I'm warning you. God did not bless me with the spirit of patience. Only the power of lead and flame."

Wooden splinters sprayed high, then fluttered to land as embers in their hair and on their shoulders.

"I'm warning you, I ain't going to be nice for long." Spivey yelled again and took aim.

Todd jeered. "Come redeem us from wickedness."

"Go home, Flint! You have no quarrel here." Jemima called out. "And you, Bill Todd, you should be ashamed of yourself."

"Oh Jemima! Two holes for two corpses." Spivey sniggered, firing off three more rapid shots. "Now it makes sense. How thoughtful of you, preach."

Rising after automatically ducking low, Dan looked at Jemima. He wiped away the wood flakes and smiled, and then he turned back towards the door and volunteered. "Throw down your gun and I'll come out."

"Think me a fool, preach? I know you're armed." Spivey emptied the pistol chamber with another three shots, then he immediately began to reload.

"You can't go out there. He's crazy." Jemima angled her body and pressed it between Dan and the door. "And if he doesn't get lucky, Bill is an excellent shot."

Dan deliberated his options. He had hoped Spivey's drunken fury would abate as it did on the first night, but this time, with the fire bombs at the ready, he knew the menace was not for turning, at least not until he had inflicted irreversible damage to the church.

"I've got to do something before they burn this place down."

"No. You must stay here with me. I've already let too many men that I've cared for walk blindly into death. I will not let that happen again." She pressed her hand against his chest until her arms were rigid.

"One last warning. Come out or I'll burn you out."

Dan diverted his eyes over Jemima's shoulder. He saw Spivey remove his Kepi and smile at Todd. Then, after scratching his head and keeping his eyes fixed on the church, he removed the cigar from behind his ear to draw smoke and liven the glowing burn. With a mouth-stretching smile, he arched and lowered the cigar to the rag-topped bottle.

Once the flame was established, Spivey shouted, "Is it not said that God is a consuming fire!" He then tossed the bottle towards the church and laughed so fiercely that his body folded at the waist.

"And Mark sayeth, for everyone will be salted by fire." Todd joined in the laughter as he watched the glass shatter against the church frontage and flames erupt in all directions.

Dan instantly grabbed Jemima and pulled her towards him in a spin that placed himself between her body and the door, then as another succession of rapid shots thudded into and through the wooden slats, he dropped to the floor taking Jemima with him. Raging flames crackled the wood and orange shafts of light pierced through the bullet holes. Dan's face twisted worryingly as, kneeling by her side, he felt hot blood ooze onto his hands.

"You're hit." His eyes bulged frantically as he saw a painful grimace on Jemima's face.

"I think I'm ok." She gasped, quickly pressing her hand on the intense burning pain in her shoulder.

Dan eased her up slightly from the floor and, kneeling beside her, he felt around her back for blood as shots continued to thud and shatter the wood about them.

"It's gone straight through." He said, feeling hot liquid close to her nape. "Can you move?"

"With a little help." She winced.

Ignoring the crackle of flame and the blasts of lead above his head, Dan delicately slipped one arm under Jemima's knees and his other around her shoulders, then with angered force, he rose from his knees and carried her towards the handcrafted pews. After gently lowering her into a recumbent position, Dan took off his coat and padded it around her body, then with hastened strides he disappeared into the blackness at the rear of the church.

"What are you doing?" She flinched, rising from the waist with alarm.

"We've got to get out of here." He replied, loading the old pistol. "You need the doctor."

"Someone will help us." She said with little faith. "God will send help."

"God sent me." He clamped the bullet cylinder and levelled the pistol in the direction of the flames to stare along his arm and the sights.

"And God will send you to the grave if you go out there alone."

He secured the pistol in his waist belt. "Sometimes you cannot teach a person the journey you believe they should take, especially when they are beyond the command of God."

"You mustn't go out there." She shook her head several times and held out her hand.

Recognising her plea, he knelt by her side again and clasped his fingers tight around her trembling hand.

"Jemima, I now understand that what I have been praying for will never come to this town whilst Spivey and his cronies live." His mind was fixed. "No matter how much I pray and seek out God's wisdom, they will not change their cruel ways."

Noticing tears wetting her cheeks, he gripped her hand tighter and wiped dry her cheek gently with the back of his left knuckle. "I now know I can never be able to rid the devil from their souls with just words and prayers."

"Spivey will kill you." She sobbed. "He does not fear God."

"Jemima, there was once a time when every sin I preach against I was guilty of. I was not raised in love and peace, nor taught to show kindness and forgiveness. I've tried real darn hard over the years to change my ways, but when my mind's turned even God's will and all his might will not stop me."

He gently touched the rear of her shoulder. Her clothes and his coat were sodden with blood. She was bleeding fast, and he knew he must hurry if he was to save her. Tenderly, he stroked her hair as he confessed.

"I wasn't born for great things and I never expected them. My troubles in the past taught me wicked ways and cursed me." She raised her face and as the flames danced off his face she noticed a meanness brace his features and banish the geniality of his nature. Now she saw it again, the beastly demon in his pupil. "Now I will use my curse to rid this town forever of its nuisance." She turned away and closed her eyes, praying silently for God's intervention as he continued to explain his motivation. "I could try every day, work hard and pray for the likes of Spivey and Dandridge, but what this town needs and what God wants are different. I see that now and it is clear what I must do." "No... no." Still hearing his words, she returned her eyes upon him. "You are angry and in your haste, they will kill you."

Suddenly and unexpectedly she lunged forward and wrapped her arms around him to hold and pull him tight against her body.

"Please let there be no more killing." She held the embrace and whispered in his ear. "Not tonight. Stay here with me a while longer. Spivey and Todd will go home and we can repair the church."

Although shocked by her unexpected affection, Dan gave her a replicated hug equally. At first, he was confused, and he suspected she was vulnerably emotional due to her long sufferings and the trauma, so he cradled her with respect, almost childlike.

However, her squeeze strengthened and her arms tightened around his back, telling him everything he once longed for, but also feared.

In his past isolation as a preacher, he had been driven into a relationship with Nettie for the strength he displayed for the Almighty. This loyalty turned into a torment and a struggle which tested him daily to be strong and patient. Now did he read signs of despairing compulsion from a woman he secretly admired?

"Jemima, this Johnny preacher can't turn their minds and everyone knows it now." He slid the gun from his belt and inspected it one last time in the firelight. "If I build another church they will turn it back into ashes."

"Please, Dan. I'm begging you to put away the gun."

"If I don't come back, it is God's will."

He levered a gap between their bodies, and in her eyes, he saw her soul reveal a yearning to be protected and loved. In that moment, he knew they both wanted the same thing, but he also knew to lead her out of the lost distress he must first deliver swift violence.

"They will kill you." Tears rolled down her cheek.

"Oh, there's going to be some killing, Jemima." He feathered his hand across her cheek, wiping away the wetness.

"You can't go. I need you. Issy needs you. You are the fire that has given us warmth and hope which has been so long missing in our lives. You steady my heart in a way I have needed for so long."

"Jemima, sometimes our hearts can't control what the mouth says." Even though he yearned for her, the sudden and emotional outcry had caught him unprepared. "Your words bring out a deep pain that I long since buried and so desperately fear."

Embarrassed by the betrayal of her emotions, Jemima let her body sag, her arms dropped loose by her side.

Sensing she had acted inappropriately, she pressed her finger gently onto his lips to indicate he should say no more.

As an awkward silence crept between them, Jemima angled her face away from him and he took a step backwards.

As he walked forward for a moment, he studied the flames which were now burning through the frontage and spreading higher towards the roof. The doorway was still clear of heat, but swirling thick smoke was beginning to bellow and, falling thick, it irritated his throat and stung his eyes. He knew there must be no further delay.

Sobbing into her hands, but looking through her fingers in the direction of the shadow, Jemima pleaded. "I'm begging you one last time. Please don't go out there."

"There may be no path to salvation for me." He shook his head briefly, recalling his past sins. "Nor may I find my place in heaven, but this has got to end. My flesh and heart may fail tonight, but God is faithful and he will restore your strength and hope."

"If those devils out there see the gun, it will give them a reason to kill you."

"When you're in hell, sometimes only the devil can get you out."

He glanced over his shoulder and smiled at Jemima, then he kicked the door outwards with the flat of his sole.

"At last the devil comes out of his lair!" Spivey shouted at the preacher, who appeared out of the smoke. Todd grinned and with one hand he swung the rifle from his shoulder and spun it in the direction of the shadow.

Dan cleared his lungs by gulping in mouthfuls of the cool night air, and from his position on the steps he looked down at the villains with contempt and condemnation. He recalled Jemima's warning about Todd's accuracy.

"Harrow hell and you rake up the devil!" Dan warned, levelling the old pistol.

"Just a mortal with a gun that bleeds like the rest of us." Spivey grinned, the flames casting a jaundiced light across his manic face.

In a flash, three blasts erupted and Todd was hurled into eternity whilst his reciprocating bullet veered high and wide into the darkness. Dan's quick fire and his aim were true, but as Spivey's lead tore a deep rut along the side of his cheek, he recoiled and momentarily staggered.

Within an instant again, both pistols lit up the street and thundered. Wood thudded behind Dan and mud splattered at Spivey's feet.

Death loomed as without delay more destructive shots were repeatedly fired. Blood belched out of Spivey's chest and he dropped to his knees, his hands dropping loose by his side. Dan adjusted his aim as he leapt from the top step.
"Drop the gun." He shouted as he quickly inspected the wound on his face with his left hand, then walking determinedly forward and keeping the barrel pointed at the bleeding man, he raged again for him to obey his command.

Spivey spat out blood instead of words and, impelled by hate and disregarding any hope of mercy, he gathered all his strength into one mighty effort and raised his pistol at the nearing duellist.

Without hesitation or remorse, Dan pulled hard on the trigger again to hurl a ball of lead deep into Spivey's forehead. His head snapped back, then slammed forward and his chin dropped onto his chest, his face immediately void of all vitality. Blood poured from his mouth and his body sagged, then slowly his arm lowered and, falling over onto his side, he released the gun.

For a moment Dan held his aim and as he kicked the discarded pistol away, he watched the dying man squirm and twitch until blood filled his lungs and his breathing waned, as he ebbed agonisingly into oblivion.

Dan raised his eyes to the darkness above and faintly muttered, "Thank you for helping me purify this town from all its unrighteousness."

Dandridge did not need to unholster his pistol. He had been impatiently waiting to discharge his cowardly slaughter from the safety of the dark boardwalk and so he was set and ready.

Leaning forward to fix his aim, an evil smirk stretched across his face as he watched the pastor stride across the mud and halt in front of Spivey to present himself as a perfect target.

Dandridge squinted through his glasses and firmed his aim at the statuesque silhouette in the glow of the flames.

With pistol roar still reverberating in his ears, the pastor did not hear the click of Dandridge's hammer, but the flash and the sounding eruption of lead to his side caused him to instinctively, but futilely, twist and swing round his pistol. Without time to return fire, an intense bolt of pain in his chest thrust the pastor sideways and, losing all coordination, he stumbled backwards.

With senses scrambled and his vision blurred, he staggered and lost his balance. His numb fingers released his gun to the floor, and then slowly his body dropped to the mud with an uncontrolled thud.

He tried to pant rapidly to fill his lungs and regain his breath, but he had to lock his jaw against the spasms of riveting pain.

He could not hear the mocking words of the approaching gunman, but his failing consciousness recognised the orange reflection of his glasses.

He knew he had been ambushed and his life was in jeopardy, however pain ensured he could not intervene with God's destiny. Dandridge laughed and waved his pistol threateningly at the stricken man who could not rise himself out of the mud. "Poor Bill's sister was right when she warned us." Dandridge shouted to the silent faces that, disturbed by the ruckus, now began to gather in the darkness. "The apostle who recites by the power of a gun is no stranger to the smell of gunpowder, she said."

Too afraid to stop the murder, the weak and the burdened of South Cave hid from view their shamed identities and kept their distance.

The blackness of the night and the radiance of the rampant flames conquered all of Dan's remaining clarity and he repeatedly clasped his eyelids tight and reopened them to clear his vision, however he could not hold still the spinning figure who stepped out of the darkness and into the glow of the furnace.

With the grim reaper approaching fast, Dan summoned all his strength and stretched out his fingers towards his gun, but he could only brush the oak handle as the inhibiting pain in his chest caused him to retract his arm quickly and force him to press his palm over the blood-seeping wound.

"Whoever sheds the blood of a man, by a man, shall his blood be shed. Genesis 9:6." Dandridge versed loudly as he neared his victim. Then, striding above Dan, he smiled and slanted his head at a slight angle as he proudly revelled and savoured his moment of victory and execution.

Pointing his pistol downwards and directing it at the lame preacher's head, he drew a large breath and grinned as he prepared to unleash the final savage shot, but as he began to squeeze on the trigger his facial expression suddenly changed from a manic grin of supreme confidence and exultation to a grimace of perplexed shock.

His eyes bulged open with fear and panic, his jaw sagged loose and his mouth gaped wide.

Speculation danced in his probing eyes, but he had no time to react as a knife blade plunged hard and deep into his back, only stopping when the metal tip would go no further. A high-pitched scream of pain lanced everyone's ears as Dandridge spat out air and twisted his neck to face the attacker to his rear.

He could find no words and, unable to respond in any way other than casting a look of horror, he wavered on his unsteady legs until they finally gave way and he dropped to his knees. Scowling at his attacker with disbelief, he toppled over onto his back. With his eyes wide open and blood oozing from his mouth, the sweat of fear beaded on his forehead as he lay static with his life ebbing away.

"Whoever takes the life of an innocent shall be put to death." Issy calmly said. "Leviticus 24:17." Then she dropped the blood-dripping knife.

"Issy, your ma is hurt." Dan roused Issy from her trance-like state by yelling and pointing towards the inferno which was now spreading near to the main double door. "You must help me get her out of the church." He winced and coughed.

Without hesitation or consideration for danger, Issy sprang towards the steps and disappeared into the church before Dan could summon the strength to stagger up onto his knees.

Pressing his hand against the hole in his chest, he staggered slowly toward the heat that reddened his face. He paused and arched over the steps rail to regain his breath before bracing himself for the climb.

Grimacing, he dragged up one foot on the step, but to his surprise as he looked through the swirling blaze and rising cinders, he saw Jemima and Issy appear before him.

Leaning on each other for support, they stretched out their arms to embrace Dan into their huddle.

With a huge grin, Jemima longed, "Now your work here can begin."

"You think?" Dan groaned, holding one arm around Jemima and his other pressed hard against the geyser of blood on his chest.

"You are needed here." Issy declared.

"We need you." Jemima settled.

"Then never again will the wicked of this town cause you pain." His eyes told the truth.

From the violence fell a palette of peacefulness and a surreal stillness, which was only interrupted by the spit and crackle of burning wood.

No one stepped forward to offer the wounded any help, and no one rushed to inspect the three dead menaces. Alone, the cripples leaned against each other for support as they staggered away from the furnace and towards Jemima's cabin, their long shadows casting a chilling veil across the lifeless damned.

Other Westerns by Daniel Carlson include;

The Vengeance Trail

The Return

Life Taker - The Story of the Gun

A Kiss for the Cursed

The Life and Death of My Best Friend, Davy Crockett

The Betryal

The Badge and the Bullet